Oh, I Do Like To Be . . .

Also by Marie Phillips

Gods Behaving Badly
The Table of Less Valued Knights

Oh, I Do Like To Be . . .

Marie Phillips

Unbound

This edition first published in 2019

Unbound
6th Floor Mutual House,
70 Conduit Street,
London W1S 2GF

www.unbound.com

Text Design by Ellipsis, Glasgow

A CIP record for this book is available from the British Library

ISBN 9 78-1-78352-675-8 (trade pbk)
ISBN 978-1-78352-677-2 (ebook)
ISBN 978-1-78352-676-5 (limited edition)

Printed in Great Britain by CPI Group (UK) Ltd, Croydon, CR0 4YY

For all the seaside towns I've known and loved

1.

It was a hot day in the summer, one of those days that glimmers like a mayfly, only to be trampled under the heels of an unseasonal downpour twenty-four hours later. Eleanor was staring at the parking ticket on the windscreen of her car. (Eleanor is not the most important person in this story, but without her the story could not have happened, and so this is where we begin.) Eleanor's car was once an exclusive model, but it was too old and run-down to turn any heads now. Even the traffic warden beside Eleanor could see that this was a metaphor.

'But I'm legally parked,' said Eleanor. This was not the beginning of the conversation.

'Residents' parking until 6 p.m.,' repeated the traffic warden.

'But it doesn't say that,' said Eleanor.

'It does,' said the traffic warden, 'on that sign, and that one, and that one, and that one, and that one.'

'But not above this bay,' said Eleanor.

'There's the paint that marks the bay,' said the traffic warden, 'and there's the hole in the pavement where the sign used to be,

1

before some kids kicked it down. You can extrapolate.'

Had the day been less hot, had the parking ticket been more fair, Eleanor might have noticed the traffic warden's use of the word 'extrapolate' and wondered what kind of a person he was. This was the kind of thing that usually interested Eleanor. But not when she was looking down the barrel of a £35 fine (£70 if not paid within fourteen days, which she had no intention of doing).

'I'm not paying it,' she said.

'That's your prerogative,' said the traffic warden, and turned to leave.

Eleanor found this unsatisfactory.

'I'll report you,' she said, 'for overzealous ticketing.'

'Be my guest,' said the traffic warden, walking away.

'What's your badge number?'

The traffic warden ignored her.

'Hey! What's your badge number?'

She ran after the traffic warden, feeling heavy and uncomfortable in the wrong clothes for the weather: tweed trousers, a synthetic blouse already patched under the arms with sweat. She grabbed the traffic warden by the elbow.

'Oi!' said the traffic warden. 'Let go!'

But Eleanor refused to let go. There was a brief, undignified tussle, during which the traffic warden's sleeve was undeniably ripped, and possibly – though Eleanor would deny this – he also received a kick in the right shin.

She'd never find her son now, Eleanor thought later,

slumped in the back of the police car. Her children, she corrected herself. She tended to forget about Sally.

2.

At the far end of the not-very-large town, Billy and his sister Sally had just stepped off the train. Although Sally was smaller than Billy, she was wearing the oversized rucksack, while Billy dragged the case on wheels, because of his back. There was nothing wrong with Billy's back, but it was important that it stayed that way.

'What do you think?' said Billy.

They looked around the station car park. There were several parked cars, and a cab rank with a waiting cab, the window half rolled down and a curl of cigarette smoke emanating above the 'No Smoking' sticker on the glass. Here and there the tarmac was cracked and some weeds poked through. There was a thin layer of sand on top of everything, and an angry seagull perched on a lamp post, although seagulls always looked angry, thought Billy. He wondered whether this counted as an original observation.

'I like it,' said Sally, which was the right answer. Billy smiled.

'Why don't you take both bags,' he said, 'and find us a B&B? I'll head to the beach, soak up the atmosphere, get the old creativity going . . . Rolling,' he corrected himself, liking the feel of the word on his tongue, thinking it was a better word, and then changing his mind, 'going' was better, less try-hard.

Sally headed off up the hill into town, the huge rucksack above her short, stocky legs making her look like a dung beetle, thought Billy. Although didn't dung beetles carry the dung balls upside-down? Maybe he meant another type of beetle. A scarab. But then beetles' legs were spindly, not stocky. No matter what the type. So he probably didn't mean a beetle at all. She just looked like Sally, carrying a big rucksack and pulling the wheelie case behind her.

The beach wasn't far from the station. Even on a Friday it was packed, being the school holidays. Billy stood at the top of the strand wondering whether or not to take his trainers off. Walking on the beach in shoes felt wrong, but he hated putting his socks and shoes back on sandy feet, and he could never get all the sand off no matter how much he tried. Then the sand would get everywhere in his room at the B&B and, later, if they moved into a flat, it would somehow get there too, spreading and spreading like . . . Germs? Butter? The Mongol hordes of Genghis Khan? Was that racist?

He decided to take his shoes and socks off anyway. If he wasn't going to feel the sand beneath his feet, he may as well not have come.

He walked towards the water. The sand was scorching underfoot, but even so he enjoyed the way it felt, the soft yielding and yet also the firmness beneath, the slight crunch. He scanned the horizon, took in the rise and fall of the waves, the pounding as they hit the shore, the inchoate cries of the seagulls as they swooped above – yes, he told himself, yes, this is it, finally, the place where I can write! But it was impossible to ignore the all-too-choate sounds of the human beings around him: babies screaming, kids demanding ice creams, teenagers pleading to go to the arcade, husbands and wives arguing over who forgot to bring the sunscreen. Also, he wasn't sure that 'choate' was a word. It should be. If Shakespeare can make up words, he thought, so can I.

This made him think of his mother. He checked the pockets of his shorts. He had just enough change either for an ice cream or for a postcard and a stamp. He did send his mother postcards, so that she would know he was still alive. He tried to choose ones that were vague enough, that didn't give the name of the town he was staying in. He never wrote much on the postcards. He couldn't bear to think of her picking them apart, making comparisons, the way she used to with his school essays. A few generic phrases were enough. So that she would know he hadn't bothered to try.

He decided on an ice cream. There was a booth up beside the road. The woman inside greeted him with warm familiarity. People often thought that they knew him, but they never knew from where. Billy knew. The muddy hair, already at thirty-two fast receding from the domed forehead; the round eyes, brown, settling a 500-year-old debate; the goatee beard, which he could have shaved off, but which undeniably suited his face shape; the small, soft lips, ever-ready to pronounce great wisdom: they'd seen his face hundreds of times before, on

7

books, posters, mugs, tote bags, T-shirts, novelty soaps . . . It was surprising how infrequently anyone ever remarked on it. But then who expects to run into William Shakespeare chewing on the gooey end of a 99 Flake?

He wandered back towards the sea. He imagined himself stripping off (maybe just to underwear; even in these last moments he wouldn't want to embarrass himself) and swimming out as far as he could, and then farther, until he exhausted himself, went under. The authorities might even think it was an accident. They said that drowning was a good way to go, although God knows who 'they' were. He doubted very much that people who had been brought round after almost drowning said, 'That was great! I really want to do that again.' It was just something that people said at parties, people who had no idea whether or not it was true. He was a cliché even for thinking it. And also, he was a strong swimmer. He might get farther than he expected. He might reach France. Then, there he would be, alive, in France, wearing only his pants (just as well he'd decided to keep them on). There were so many things to consider. To be or not to be? Even contemplating suicide, that bastard had got there first.

Probably, he conceded, he would not reach France.

He imagined Sally coming down to the beach and looking for him. He pictured her finding his clothes in a pile, and waiting beside them for him to come back. Looking out to sea, trying to spot the dot that was his head. How long would she wait before she started to worry? To panic? And then, after-wards, how long before she didn't miss him any more?

8

The melting ice cream dripped onto his hand. He should have bought the postcard.

'There you are!'

Billy looked up and saw Sally approaching him along the waterfront.

'That was quick,' he said.

Sally frowned.

'Do you want one?' Billy said, holding up the ice cream. 'You can have the rest of mine if you like. I'm not in the mood.'

Sally hesitated, then grinned. 'OK!' she said.

Billy handed the ice cream over. Sally took a cheerful lick.

'It didn't take you long to find somewhere,' he said.

That frown again.

'I'll get writing soon,' he reassured her. 'I just had to take in my surroundings first.'

Sally's frown deepened. 'You shouldn't be writing now,' she said. 'You're late for lunch. Thandie sent me to get you. And you shouldn't be eating ice cream either, but that's OK, because you're not.' She grinned again and took another lick of the ice cream.

'Thandie?'

'Yes. She's really angry.'

Rather than explain who Thandie was, Sally turned and headed back up to the road. Billy pulled on his shoes and socks, feeling the unpleasant rasp of the sand over his skin – wrong decision again – and ran after her. Thandie must be the landlady at the B&B. Sally had obviously picked somewhere with full board, forgetting the rules they'd established after the

Great Food Poisoning Incident of Barrow-in-Furness. Why would this Thandie be angry, though? What had Sally done? It was true that people often got frustrated with Sally, but rarely actually angry.

'But you think it's OK, though?' he asked her as they trotted along, past shops selling boogie boards and buckets and spades and miniature castles built from shells.

'What?'

'The place.'

'Of course it is,' said Sally. 'It's lovely.'

Lovely? That didn't sound right.

'We can afford it, right?'

Sally turned to him, worried. 'Gosh, I hope so,' she said.

Billy felt a stab of guilt. It was Sally's money, earned at a variety of low-paid jobs in the towns that they stopped in, that paid their B&B bills, not to mention all their other expenses. Billy intended to make up for this once one of his plays was produced, which would mean first finishing a play. His thoughts drifted reluctantly towards the half-filled notebooks in the wheelie bag at the B&B, the fragmentary thoughts and phrases that never cohered into anything, like that jelly Eleanor had tried to make for his birthday once, a sweet, viscous liquid that swam around in its rabbit-shaped mould but never set. In the end they'd drunk it all the same. Was that a good image? Maybe. Was it Shakespeare-good, though?

Sally weaved her way through the streets of the town as though she lived there. Billy hurried to keep up, surprised at her sudden competence. How had she managed to find somewhere to stay so quickly, and so far off the beaten track? Usually they lodged on one of those strips where every building is a guest house more dispiriting than the last, where it feels like a minor triumph if your bedroom has a sink with a hot tap. The area Sally led them to now was uphill from the shopping district, a warren of low stone cottages with a faded charm and a view of the sea. It was, in a word, nice. That was new.

'This is a good, solid town,' Billy observed. 'It's not run-down enough to be depressing, but nor is it all gentrified and . . .' Intimidating, was the word that popped into his mind. He decided not to say it. 'I feel like this is somewhere we could really belong, you know?' he said instead.

'We do belong here,' said Sally.

'Oh. Yeah. Maybe, yeah. That's really optimistic of you, Sally. Good attitude.'

Sally peered at him. 'You're acting weird today, Bill.'

'Well, you know, there's always an adjustment period.'

'Saying things like that. That's exactly what I mean.'

'Yes, well, you're acting weird too.'

Sally shrugged and, having finished the ice cream, licked the remnants off her fingers. Then she suddenly turned and skipped up the steps to a small grey cottage with a neatly tended garden in the front. Billy looked around. There wasn't any kind of sign that it was a B&B.

'Sally,' he said, 'you didn't just meet someone in the street who invited you to come home with them? You can't trust people like that. They could rob us, or worse.'

11

'Of course not,' said Sally. 'Not after last time. Whoo! That was scary.'

'What last time?' said Billy.

'If it hadn't been for that passing policeman,' said Sally, ringing the doorbell, 'I'd have been in a whole lot of trouble, but don't worry, I've learned my lesson, never gonna do that again.'

'What last time?' said Billy again, but as he spoke the door opened, revealing a strikingly beautiful and even more strikingly annoyed-looking woman on the threshold.

3.

'Thandie?' said Billy.

She had long, curling black hair, huge eyes, and the kind of voluptuous body Billy would happily move into.

'About bloody time too,' she said.

'I'm sorry?' said Billy.

'So you should be. Glad you made it at long last.'

There didn't seem much he could say to that. He offered: 'Yes.'

Thandie turned and headed back into the house, Sally close behind her and, after a moment, Billy followed her in too. The entrance hall was surreal: nothing like the places they usually stayed, it had pale-blue William Morris wallpaper and a few framed botanical prints, and no signs of mould. It was – he searched for the right word – pleasant. He was uncomfortably aware of tracking sand on the polished floorboards.

Thandie rooted around in a handbag on the hall table and pulled out a £20 note which she handed to Sally with a heart-melting smile.

'I need to talk to Bill alone, love,' she said. 'Why don't you head down to the pub?'

'Thanks, Thandie,' said Sally, appearing pleased but not surprised. 'See you later!' And with that she went back out, shutting the door behind her. What kind of a place was this, where the landlady handed out cash?

Meanwhile, Thandie was walking ahead of him, the rear view as good as the front. She headed through a wood-panelled door into a room at the back of the cottage. 'And don't you start about me giving money to Sal,' she was saying. 'I know you won't approve, but she doesn't have much, and she's out of work, and she's feeling so down about it . . . What can I tell you, I'm a soft touch.'

Sally had a knack of making friends quickly, reflected Billy. He, less so.

He followed Thandie into a living room running the width of the house, with French doors open onto a sunny patio, bursting with plants. At one end of the room was a round table, set for two.

'I cooked, like an idiot,' she said. 'I actually thought it might be nice, for us to share a meal together, while we talk things through.'

Billy tried to remember if he'd ever been offered so much as a Mint Imperial while previous landladies had detailed how to unblock the shower drain and that towels would only be changed every other week.

'It will be nice,' he said.

'Well then, why weren't you here any earlier?'

This woman's moodiness was incomprehensible.

'I came as soon as I knew you were waiting.'

'The chicken'll be dry now,' said Thandie, ducking through a door into what presumably was the kitchen. 'You could at least try to keep to our arrangements.'

'Yes,' said Billy. 'I will in future. This is a lovely house, by the way.'

There was a long silence, and then Thandie said, in a peculiar tone, 'I know.' Then she added, 'I'm just going to make the gravy.'

Billy wandered around the living room, asking himself what kind of a deal Sally could possibly have struck to allow them to stay in such a swanky place. As well as the dining table, there was a comfortable-looking sofa with a matching armchair, both with all their springs and stuffing still inside them. Against one wall stood a polished upright piano, with a few framed photographs displayed on top. The other walls were lined with bookshelves, and instead of the torn-jacketed Jeffrey Archer novels and *Shades of Grey* sequels he was used to – when the places where they stayed had books at all – there were classic novels, modern prize-winners, volumes of plays and poetry. He spotted several of his favourites, a few of which he had stolen from libraries in towns they'd passed through and were now stuffed in the wheelie bag. He couldn't have asked for a better living room if he had designed it himself.

'Do you want wine?' said Thandie from the kitchen. 'I know I could do with some.'

Since when did these places serve wine? Maybe this Thandie was an alcoholic – that would certainly explain a lot. Still, Billy had never been one for examining the mouths of gift horses. 'That would be great,' he said. 'Thank you.'

Near the French doors, there was a stylish wooden rocking chair with a low table beside it, this one tottering with books – exactly the kind of chair that Billy would love to sit in and read. He glanced towards the kitchen door, but there was no sign of Thandie returning.

'Mind if I sit?' he said.

'Of course not,' said Thandie in that peculiar tone again.

Billy lowered himself into the rocking chair and leaned back. It was the perfect height for him, with just the right amount of give. He reached over and took the top book off the pile on the table. It was a play, called *If You Say So*, by one William Evans. He turned it over to read the back cover, shrieked and dropped the book.

Thandie rushed in from the kitchen, brandishing a wooden spatula. 'Are you all right?'

'Yes, I . . .' Billy picked up the book and clapped his hand down over the photo on the back. 'I thought I saw a mouse.'

'Oh, God, yes, you probably did. I do keep saying we should get a cat. Close the patio doors if you like. Christ, you nearly gave me a heart attack. I'll just be a minute.'

Thandie headed back into the kitchen. Billy peeled his hand off the back of the book and looked down at what was quite clearly a photograph of himself, sitting in this very chair in this very room, a room that he had never been in before today.

Trembling, Billy got up and went over and examined the bookshelves. He found a whole shelf of plays and poetry by William Evans and, when he pulled out a couple, they had the same photograph on the back, the photo of him. Time seemed simultaneously to slow down and speed up. He lurched over to the piano and scanned the photos until he found what he was looking for. He picked it up: a silver-framed portrait of Thandie in a wedding dress, a veil pushed back over her long, dark hair. She was laughing, and her eyes were filled with love as she gazed over at the man on her arm, who was, of course, himself. Or rather, William Evans. Another himself. Another Shakespeare.

Thandie came in carrying two glasses of wine, saying, 'I thought I'd open that bottle your father gave us.' Father? His mother had always said that she hadn't needed a man; all she'd needed was a womb, a laboratory and one of Shakespeare's wisdom teeth. And now he had a father? Who was he? An ex-husband? Another scientist? A clone of William Shakespeare's actual dad? Argh, he hated the word 'clone'!

'Why are you looking at that?' said Thandie.

Billy looked down at the wedding photograph in his hand, at the happy Thandie there.

'You look so beautiful,' he said.

The real Thandie's face hardened. She slammed the glasses down on the dining table. Some wine sloshed over the side of one of them. 'I'll get the chicken,' she said.

'Chicken, right,' said Billy. I need to get out of here immediately, he thought.

He tossed the photograph onto the piano and made a move for the door. Thandie came back in with a roast chicken studded with rosemary, on a bed of onions and whole roasted garlic cloves.

Well, thought Billy, maybe not quite immediately.

Thandie returned to the kitchen and emerged with a dish of crispy roast potatoes and carrots, and a steaming bowl of gravy. The smell of the food made Billy's mouth water. He could barely remember the last meal he'd eaten that hadn't come in a bun. He thought of Sally with her £20 in the pub and hoped that she was getting something just as delicious, though it was hard to imagine that she could.

Thandie looked at him and he looked at Thandie and Thandie looked at the chicken and he looked at the chicken and then he realised that Thandie was expecting him to carve. He'd never carved a chicken in his life. He wondered how much of it he could eat while still staying polite. Half the chicken had to be fine, surely. He picked up the carving knife and the long matching fork and started hacking pieces off the bird as best he could. Thandie watched for a while.

'Have you been drinking?' she said.

'No,' said Billy. Thandie seemed to require a further explanation. 'I'm just nervous,' he said.

Which was true enough. Thandie shrugged and began serving the vegetables. Billy experienced a small amount of relief in a situation that was far from relieving. Maybe he'd be able to busk his way through this. He'd gone to drama school in London, because it had seemed like the kind of thing a modern-day Shakespeare would do, and then he'd dropped out after a year to try to write, which he also told himself was appropriately Shakespearean. The truth was that he wasn't an especially good actor, but he had learned to improvise under pressure, which he hoped would keep him in good stead here. He put some mangled pieces of chicken on both plates and then poured the gravy, which looked so thick and rich that it was all he could do not to drink it straight out of the bowl.

'Cheers,' said Thandie, holding up her wine glass. Yes. Drinking wine was better than drinking gravy.

'Cheers,' said Billy.

They clinked glasses and drank, Billy a large mouthful, hoping for anaesthesia. He got something even better than that. He gasped.

'This wine is amazing!' he said.

'Well, you know your dad,' said Thandie inaccurately.

Billy began to eat, trying not to gobble. Thandie was right, the chicken was a bit dry – Billy suspected that she could have taken it out of the oven on time, but had left it in to punish him, or rather William Evans, for having been so late. Thanks a lot, William, he thought. It was still the best thing that he'd eaten in – well – years. Imagine if this was his life! His house, his wife, his shelf of published work. William Evans was the luckiest man alive. Maybe I should kill him and take his place, he thought suddenly, but no, unfortunately, he wasn't that kind of man. He just needed to eat and go. And maybe take Thandie upstairs for a good seeing to after the meal. William Evans could hardly complain, he should be grateful that he wasn't going to get murdered.

He realised that Thandie was just sitting there, watching him stuffing himself, and made an effort to slow down. He smiled at her as he chewed, attempting to show his appreciation. My God, she was gorgeous.

Thandie ate a tiny morsel of her chicken, then put her knife and fork down. Great, thought Billy, if she's not going to eat, maybe I can have the whole thing!

'Bill,' she said. 'We need to talk.'

Oh, no. No, no. These conversations were bad enough when they were about him. He certainly didn't need to take one for the William Evans team. He glanced towards the French doors, the door to the hallway. Maybe he could make a run for it.

On the other hand, the chicken.

On the other, other hand, Thandie's face.

'We need to have a serious conversation about this marriage,' said Thandie.

And here we go.

Billy had just taken a huge bite of chicken, so Thandie had to wait for quite some time while he made his way through it.

'Yes,' he said eventually. 'Absolutely. I couldn't agree more. Just not right now.'

'If we're not going to talk about it now, when are we going to talk about it?'

'Literally any other time would be better for me.'

'Oh, I'm sure it would be. If it were up to you we'd never talk about it at all. I mean, just look at today! You turn up late, you disrespect my cooking—'

'I definitely do not disrespect your cooking.'

'—hacking into it like you're cutting down a tree, you refuse to engage with me when I'm trying to talk to you about something really important—'

'Could you pass the carrots?'

'I'm doing all the work here, and you're giving me nothing.'

'And . . .' he said. 'The gravy?'

'This marriage is dead, Bill.'

The statement landed on the table with a thud. Billy tried to make the face of a person whose marriage was dead and not of someone who had just met this woman fifteen minutes previously and who was starting to ask himself what would happen when her real husband turned up.

'Don't you have anything to say about that?'

'Well, obviously, I'm very sad that the marriage is dead,' said Billy. From Thandie's expression, this wasn't good enough. 'I'm heartbroken. Devastated.' What he would give for a thesaurus. 'Inconsolable?'

'Stop being facetious.'

'I'm not. I really mean it. Let's give things another try. There's really no need for us to discuss this any further.'

'I don't know why I expected more from you,' said Thandie. 'You've never put the slightest bit of effort into our relationship. I mean, I knew from the start that your work was always going to come first – you were very clear about that, and I accepted it – but it's just got worse and worse. Lately it seems like even when you're here, you're not here.'

Thandie sounded so sorrowful that Billy found himself starting to feel guilty, even though it had nothing to do with him.

'We live in the same house, sleep in the same bed, but I don't feel like we're sharing our lives,' Thandie went on. 'You don't take any interest in me, you don't show me any affection. Our sex life is basically zero.'

Billy looked up sharply from his plate. If William Evans wasn't giving her any (more fool him), he knew someone who would.

'It's wearing me down,' Thandie continued. 'I'm not myself any more. I feel so old – I'm not old, Bill! We used to talk about having a baby, I can't even imagine that happening any more. And . . . I feel like – lately I sense that – don't deny it . . .'

Billy felt a rising sense of panic as he guessed where this was heading.

'I think you've been seeing someone else,' Thandie said finally. 'I don't have any proof, I haven't been snooping or any-thing, it's just – I can't think of any other explanation for how you've been behaving.'

Just as he'd expected. What an arsehole William Evans was! Billy had no idea what to say. He was hardly going to defend the guy. Plus he was acutely aware that his chicken was getting cold.

'I know it's partly my fault,' Thandie said. 'I know there

hasn't been much to attract you lately – but I get so exhausted by trying and failing to get your attention – and then I've got nothing left to offer – and so you go elsewhere – it's a vicious circle . . .'

Billy was outraged on Thandie's behalf. She had more than enough to offer, from where he was sitting. How could she take it all on herself when this shit William Evans was clearly entirely to blame? Ungrateful sod! He slammed his fist down on the table. Thandie jumped.

'This is appalling!' he cried. 'I have treated you dreadfully! It's all my fault – don't you dare say otherwise. Nobody should have to put up with the way I've behaved, especially you. You've been such a wonderful wife to me – patient, loving, under-standing, super-hot and great in the sack – the very idea that I would cheat on you – it's reprehensible! I'm a dog! I don't deserve you, Thandie, and I would give all my plays and books of poems and other published works to have you love me again.'

Billy meant every word of this – albeit on behalf of that animal, William Evans – but he wondered whether maybe he had laid it on a bit thick, because Thandie had a look of shock on her face, perhaps even disbelief. He quickly ate a little bit more of his chicken.

'Also,' he added, 'you're an amazing cook. Really.'

Thandie began to smile, but at that moment her phone, lying on the table beside her, rang. Thank you, God! thought Billy. Maybe this awful conversation could now come to an end.

'Go ahead,' he said, 'take it, it might be important.'

Thandie looked at the display. Her face went white.

'It's you,' she said.

I take it back, God! Billy's hand scrambled around in his pocket, hurrying to switch his phone to silent.

'Don't pick up,' he said. 'My phone was stolen earlier, that's why I was late.'

But it was too late. Thandie had already lifted the phone to her ear.

'Listen to me carefully,' she said. 'I don't know what you want, but if you ever call this number again, I'm phoning the police.'

Oh dear, thought Billy.

4.

Bill stared at his phone, aghast. This couldn't just be because he was late for lunch. Somehow, Thandie must have found out about Anthony. Well, there was no point going home now. Not without a serious rethink, of the pub variety.

The Boar's Head was an unreconstructed old-man pub that the hipsters had yet to discover and destroy. The smell of stale beer, windows that let in no light, a carpet that stuck to your feet with every step, ancient geezers in rotting jackets sitting at small round tables drinking bitter and reading the *Racing Post*, ignoring each other and yet enjoying the companionship of being ageing and cantankerous together. Bill loved the unpretentiousness of it, which he knew made him pretentious himself, but he didn't care.

Not entirely to his surprise, he spotted Sal sitting at the back of the room, with some leftover chip papers beside her, drinking a lime and soda and making her way through a pile of magazines. Sal's hobby was hobby magazines. She liked reading them and imagining having the hobbies she didn't have. Today she had fresh copies of *Angler's Mail*, *Crochet World* and *Fine Art Connoisseur*. Bill wondered where she had got the money from. He knew she'd been fired from her latest job, in the sweet shop on the high street, for giving sweets away to cute children, cute children being the main customer base of the sweet shop. He'd popped in to see her, and the manager had explained, with regret, that he'd had to let her go, even though she was a pleasure to have around the place. He was sure, he'd said, that she'd find something else. Bill wasn't so sure.

Bill got himself a whisky and ginger from the bar – the barmaid greeted him by name, another reason he liked this place – and went and sat down beside his sister.

'You all right, Sal?' he said.

'I'm learning how to make an antique-style lace shawl,' said Sal. She held up *Crochet World*.

'I heard about the job.'

'Oh. I'm sorry, Bill. I really tried this time.'

'It's OK, Sal, you don't have to apologise to me. We just need to find you something more suited to you. Maybe you can become a professional crochet-er.'

'I don't think so. It looks really hard. I think it would take me a year to make one antique-style lace shawl with . . .' She squinted at the page '. . . broderie anglaise detailing.'

'Well, don't worry. We'll think of something.' He put his arm around his sister's shoulders and gave her a squeeze.

'Thanks, bro. So. How was lunch?'

'I didn't go.'

'What?'

'I just called Thandie to apologise for running late, and she was really angry. So I haven't gone yet. Too scary.'

'But I took you there myself.'

'No, you didn't.'

'Yes, I did. Half an hour ago. Thandie gave me twenty quid.' Sal indicated the hobby magazines with her hand.

Bill frowned. Sal wasn't the sharpest pickle in the jar, true, but she wasn't delusional. She must be remembering another time, another twenty quid – Thandie giving her money was hardly unprecedented, Bill didn't think it was a good idea, it was one of the many things they argued about. But that was hardly the main issue now. Losing this job must have affected her more than she was letting on.

'Listen,' he said, 'why don't you try that newsagent that's just opened, down on the front? They might be looking for someone. You'd like that, wouldn't you? Working with magazines?'

'That's a great idea,' said Sal. 'Thanks, Bill! Are you feeling better now, by the way?'

'What do you mean?'

'You were acting really weird, earlier.'

There wasn't any earlier. But Bill didn't want to worry her, so he just said, 'Yes, I'm feeling much better.'

He knocked back his whisky and ginger, enjoyed the fizz and the burn.

'Right,' he said. 'Better go and face the music.'

Though first he was going to drop into that newsagent himself, and have a word with the owner. Not to put off seeing Thandie, obviously not. Just doing a favour for his little sis.

5.

Coming out of the newsagent, having primed the owner for Sal's arrival, Bill spotted his sister heading along the waterfront towards him. He waved her over.

'Sorry, Billy,' she said, 'that took forever.'

'Really?' said Bill. 'I thought you were very quick. Are you going in right now? I'll come with you if you like.'

'In where?'

'The newsagent.'

'Oh,' said Sally, 'I wasn't going there. I found us rooms.'

'Rooms?'

'At a B&B.'

'Why?'

'Because we need them.'

A lifetime of being Sal's brother and she was still able to surprise him. He underestimated her, he realised. He was used to thinking of her as someone he needed to help and protect. And now she was looking after him, anticipating his needs, just at the right moment. Thandie was furious this time. They had been through some rocky patches in their marriage, sure, but she had never threatened to call the police before. Of course, he couldn't go home, not with things the way they were between them. He needed space, time to figure out what to do next. And who other than Sal would realise this? Sal, who knew him better than anyone?

'Sal, you're the best,' Bill told her. 'But you don't need to come and stay with me. I'll be fine on my own.'

'Where else am I going to stay?' said Sally.

Bill was moved beyond words. He threw his arms around his sister and hugged her close.

Sally led the way to the B&B she had found. It was on a seedy strip not far from the station, a row of stucco-fronted buildings with pieces missing, like chunks of icing snaffled off a wedding cake. They all had signs outside them with names like 'Seaview Cottage' or 'Ocean Sands', despite the fact that the only water you could see from their rooms was rising damp. You could smell the sea though, that familiar tang in the air, mixed with the stench of bubbling fat from the chip shop on the corner and wafts of sour heat from the launderette next door to it.

'Most places were full,' explained Sally, 'because of it being the summer, and a weekend, but I got lucky with this one, and she's only going to charge us two pounds extra a night for the sheets.'

Sally led him up the stairs to an establishment optimistically monikered 'Shady Palms'. There wasn't a palm tree in sight. Though to be fair, it did look quite shady. Bill thought maybe he had seen it before, in a documentary about the explosion of drug use in beach towns. He began to feel a creeping sense of discomfort, as if the cockroaches he was sure were in there had come out and started crawling up his legs.

'She says not to turn the door handle, because it might come off,' said Sally, as she let them into the building using a key with a large tag shaped like a fish, 'but if you turn the key and sort of jiggle the door with your shoulder, it opens quite easily.'

The front room had been converted into a reception area, with a wood veneer desk that housed an ancient computer and a world of unfiled papers, the office chair behind which had one wheel missing and was being propped up by a phone book. Bill couldn't remember when he had last seen a phone book. This one was from 1997. The landlady of the B&B was sitting in a different chair, a high-backed padded leather, or possibly pleather, one with a tear in the arm that had been fixed with masking tape. From nowhere, Bill remembered that pleather had recently been rebranded 'vegan leather'. The chair had its back to the door and was facing a television, mounted on the wall, that was showing QVC. A woman on the screen was extolling the virtues of cubic zirconium jewellery. Bill could see six bracelets and four rings on the landlady's visible arm and hand, all featuring stones that were slightly too brightly coloured to look real.

'Hey, Violet,' said Sally, 'we're back.'

Violet got up and turned to them. She was deeply tanned and wrinkled from sun damage and might have been anywhere from forty to sixty. As well as the jewellery Bill had already seen, she also had a ring in her nose, two in her right eyebrow and several in each ear. Her hair had been twisted into dreadlocks and dyed a variety of bright colours, and she was wearing a tie-dyed caftan. Bill, thrown by the kaleidoscope of colour, said the first thing that popped into his head: 'Are you vegan?'

'No food in the rooms,' said Violet.

'No. I just meant – the chair,' said Bill.

'I'm not planning to eat it, if that's what you mean.'

'Our rooms are on the top floor,' Sally told Bill. 'They're really hot, but that's good in the winter, but it's not winter, and anyway in the winter, they're cold. But we can have the windows open when we're in our rooms. Now. Not in the winter.'

'Great,' said Bill, trying to tear his eyes away from Violet. He had just noticed that she had rings on her toes as well. He would use her in something, he knew. Bill had a weakness for writing about eccentric landladies in inns and taverns – she would transpose nicely to a tavern.

'I carried your bag up already,' said Sally. She was heading for the stairs, and Bill hurried along behind her.

'When did you have time to pack me a bag?' Bill asked.

'I didn't,' said Sally.

Of course, thought Bill, Thandie must have already packed his bags for him.

'I put you in the room at the back,' said Sally when they reached the sweltering top landing, 'because it's quieter, so you can write.'

'That's really thoughtful. This redraft is driving me mad.'

Sally stared at him, amazed. 'Redraft?'

'Of the play. *Charles II*. Though I'm worried if I call it that, people will wonder whether it's the sequel to a play called *Charles*.'

'You've written a whole play?'

'Yes. Well, no, not exactly, it only goes as far as the return from exile. So really I should call it *Charles II Part 1*, but that's going to confuse people even more.'

'Can I read it?'

'When I've finished it, of course.'

Now it was Sally's turn to throw her arms around him. 'I'm so proud of you,' she said. 'I know how hard it's been, comparing yourself to Shakespeare all the time, but I knew you'd get there.'

Bill was surprised, again, at Sal's insight. He'd never discussed it with her, the pain he felt at all the Shakespeare comparisons in his reviews: 'derivative', 'a pale copy', 'too in thrall to Shakespeare'. He didn't try to write like Shakespeare, it just came out that way. It shouldn't be a bad thing, but you try telling that to newspaper critics.

'I don't even like Shakespeare,' added Sally. 'All those words.'

Bill thought of remonstrating with her, then thought better of it. Another time.

She detached herself from him and handed over his room key, which had a tag shaped like a lobster. It was very pink and there was a little hole where its eye had fallen out.

'You'll be all right here for a while, won't you?' she said. 'I need to start looking for a job.'

'I'll be fine,' said Bill. 'Great attitude. Straight back on the horse. You've been fantastic today. Don't forget that newsagent on the front, will you?'

Sally looked confused, but she nodded. 'Newsagent,' she said. 'Right.'

She headed back down the stairs, while Bill unlocked the door to his room. A new cloud of heat hit him, rich and damp and smelling of mushrooms. He went into the room without closing the door behind him, and tried to open the window. Eventually it grudgingly budged, and Bill noticed that there was some kind of exhaust from the launderette next door, belching steam directly beside it. He hastily shoved the window back down again, hoping it wasn't toxic.

The room had a thick royal blue carpet, curling up at the corners. The single bed had a matching thick blue coverlet, with miscellaneous stains. The curtains, which might have been of use had they too been thick and blue, were flimsy and a once-white grey, and hung unevenly where some of the plastic hooks had snapped. The wallpaper was shiny and white with little blue flowers, and there was a huge patch of yellow-brown damp colonising the wall opposite the bed. There was no bathroom, but at the foot of the bed was a ceramic sink with a single, dripping cold tap. Beneath the sink was an over-stuffed wheelie case that he didn't recognise. It was in a terrible state – must have been the worst piece of luggage that Thandie could dig out of the loft, another signal of her contempt for him. He hesitated in front of it, uncertain whether to unpack into this repellant cesspit – was this really the best that Sal could find? – or to give up on his posturing and head home. If that was even an option now.

It's all material, he tried to tell himself. Just think how much more convincingly I'll be able to write about degradation now that I've been so thoroughly degraded. Oh God, he was probably inhaling spores! He didn't want to hurt Sal's feelings, but neither did he want to die tragically young of a fungal respiratory disease. He needed to make a decision: stay or go home. To B&B or not to B&B? That was the question.

Maybe there was a third option. He texted Anthony: 'You free for a drink?'

Then he found the least stained section of the coverlet and sat down – very gingerly – to wait.

6.

After Bill's phone call, even the combined attractions of Thandie and the chicken weren't enough to keep Billy in the cottage. His doppelgänger might be home any minute. He mentally bid a sorry farewell to the rest of his lunch, then told Thandie he needed a walk to clear his head. He allowed himself the luxury of using the pristine bathroom before he left. He had actually forgotten that not all bathrooms are a biohazard. Then he took one last look at Thandie. For that moment, he considered staying, but he knew there was no way this could end well for him.

Once out under the beating sun, Billy traced his way back down the hill towards the waterfront, and let his thoughts catch up with him. There was another Shakespeare out there. Maybe even more than one. Who knew how many Eleanor had created? He had always known that he was not unique, that he was merely a reproduction of the great original, but he had taken some solace in being the only Shakespeare copy, the only one who knew what it was like to be him – to be Him. Through failure after failure he'd told himself that it wasn't his fault, that the circumstances of his creation had made his life impossible, that nobody could withstand the intolerable pressure of trying to live up to such expectations. And now he discovered that not only was there another living Shakespeare, the other one was a success!

His hand hovered over his pocket, wondering if he should break five years of silence and call his mother, but he was overwhelmed with the familiar shame of how much he had disappointed her, and then the anger associated with that shame, and so he didn't call. (It wouldn't have made any difference if he had, as his mother was currently in a police cell less than twenty minutes' walk away, awaiting processing for assault on a traffic warden, and her phone had been confiscated, along with her shoes and belt.)

He needed a drink, he decided. He looked around for a pub, rejected a couple for being too chichi and finally settled on a place called the Boar's Head, which had a pleasingly unpolished air. Very him, he thought. He went inside, returned the barmaid's friendly hello and spotted Sally sitting at the back of the room, reading a magazine about fishing. Perfect. He remembered that he didn't have any money on him, but that Sally did.

'Hey, sis,' he said, 'shout me a pint?'

He sat down in the other chair at her table while she went and got them both a drink. He flicked through the pile of magazines she'd been looking at. Weird selection. This didn't seem like the kind of pub that would have a subscription to *Fine Art Connoisseur*.

Sal came back with the drinks.

'We've got to leave town,' Billy said without preamble. 'As soon as I finish this drink.'

'But – why?' said Sal.

'There's another Shakespeare,' said Billy.

'What do you mean, another Shakespeare?'

'She must have made two. Or more. And one of them is living in that house.'

'What do you mean, made two? What house? I don't understand.'

'I'm just getting my head round it myself. And Thandie! What a woman! I can never see her again.'

'What – never?'

'I know. It's crazy. You don't meet someone like that every day. And if I could see any way of making it work – but it's hopeless. Too complicated. Better to have a clean break.'

'Just like that?'

'Yeah. We'll just – forget all about her and go.'

'But I don't want to go,' said Sal. Billy thought she looked surprisingly upset, she should be used to moving on by now. 'What about the newsagent?' she said.

'What newsagent? Don't worry about the newsagent. There are newsagents everywhere. Get our stuff together and go to the station, book us some tickets on the first train out of here, and I'll come meet you there the moment I've finished my pint.'

'Now?'

'Yes.'

'What about saying goodbye?'

'Who on earth do you want to say goodbye to?'

Sal thought of all the people she had grown up with: her father, her friends, the locals who knew her by name. Thandie, who was like a sister to her.

'OK,' she said. 'If this is what you want.' She stood up, leaving her drink untouched. 'I still think you're acting really weird today.'

'Of course I am. There's another Shakespeare.'

'Well,' said Sal, 'I suppose that is weird.'

She left the pub, her shoulders sloped with sadness.

Billy took a sip of his pint. It was good. Bittersweet, like Thandie. He wondered whether he could go and see her again, but, of course, that was impossible. William Evans was probably there already, sitting in his rocking chair, kissing his wife, eating his chicken, admiring his shelf of bestsellers.

William Evans. If the two of them were, in genetic terms at least, the same person, why had their destinies turned out so differently? By what accident had he ended up living an itinerant life, scraping by on whatever Sally could raise from zero-hours contracts in lousy jobs, unable to make anything of what he – of few people on earth – could unabashedly call his genius, while William Evans had everything he'd ever dreamed of?

He got his phone out and googled his foe, but the results – 'precocious talent', 'wunderkind', 'the theatre's hottest new sensation' – were too nauseating to pursue.

William Evans can do it, he thought. William Shakespeare could do it. So what is wrong with me?

'I thought I might find you here,' said a man's voice.

Billy looked up to see a traffic warden standing by his table.

'You're mistaking me for someone else,' he told him. 'I don't have a car.'

'Very funny,' said the traffic warden. Then, to Billy's astonishment, he leaned down and kissed him on the mouth. 'This for me?' he said, sitting down and picking up Sal's drink. 'Lime and soda? I hope there's a vodka in it. I got your text, sorry I didn't answer, I've had a hideous day. Thank God my shift is over. I got into a fight with a woman, an actual physical fight. She kicked me! I had to call the police.'

Billy stared mutely as the man pulled his cap off his pale blond hair and began to peel off his hi-vis jacket.

'Look!' he was saying. 'She tore my sleeve! I should have gone home to change but I didn't want to waste my break.'

'We're together,' Billy managed eventually. 'You and me.'

The traffic warden stopped and peered at Billy. 'Are you OK?' he said.

'I'm cheating on Thandie with you.'

'I – well, that's a bit blunt, but – yes.'

'And I'm gay.'

'I thought you didn't like labels?'

The traffic warden put his hand on Billy's, but Billy drew his away. Here was another fine mess William Evans had got him into! He decided to be direct.

41

'Listen,' he said. 'This is all a misunderstanding. I'm not who you think I am.'

The traffic warden shook his head. 'Bill, what are you saying?'

'I'm not Bill. I'm not William Evans. I'm somebody else. I look like William Evans, but I'm not him. You don't know me, and I don't know you.'

'Bill,' said the traffic warden, 'I know it hasn't been easy for you, accepting this part of you, this relationship—'

'I'm not Bill,' Billy repeated. 'Maybe it was easy for Bill. Maybe Bill is gay. I can't deny having had the odd fumble myself, there was that camping trip – that's not important right now. What I'm saying is, Bill might love you! But that's not who I am.'

'How can you say these things?' said the traffic warden.

'Because they're true. I'm not Bill.'

'Look. I don't know what kind of – of fugue state you've gone into – obviously you're struggling with your feelings, it's hard for you to deal with all the changes you're going through—'

'I'm not in a fugue state.'

'—But I thought we'd been over all this! Bill! Don't do this to me! I love you!'

The traffic warden's eyes filled with tears. He was, Billy thought, painfully young. What was William Evans playing at?

'I'm just going to say this one more time,' he said. 'I'm not Bill. And I feel very sorry for your predicament, but I've got enough on my plate without trying to sort out your relationship problems for you. Now, I'm leaving town today, and I'm in a bit of a rush. You can figure this out with Bill when you see him. Bill. Who is not me.'

Billy stood up and walked away from the table, leaving behind, with enormous regret, that pint of good beer.

'Bill!' the young traffic warden was calling after him. 'Come back! Talk to me! Bill!'

Billy pushed open the pub door and stepped out into the fierce afternoon heat.

7.

It was a nice town, thought Sally. Friendly. Even though nobody wanted to give her a job, they were all so kind to her. 'Ah, sorry love,' they said, 'we haven't got anything at the moment.' Or, 'We'd love to help, but things didn't work out so well before, now, did they? But good luck finding something.' Sally wondered what had happened before that so put these people off hiring new employees. But she didn't worry about it too much. She knew something would turn up.

Maybe now that Billy had finished a play they'd be staying in this town for a while. Sally hoped so. She was sick of travelling. Billy was special, she'd grown up knowing that, and she had to do everything she could to help him with his gift – which was a gift for the world, really, that's what their mother had always said – but she hated having to pack up and move on every few months. She wanted friends, real ones, that lasted. It felt disloyal saying that she was lonely. She and Billy had each other. But it wasn't enough for her. Even though she wasn't special, she wanted more for her life. Not that she had ever told Billy that. She didn't want to make him feel bad. But maybe, just maybe, things would be different now. Someone would put on Billy's play and it would be a big success, in the West End of London. They'd get a flat, a proper one, with two bedrooms, not one bedroom for Billy and the sofa in the living room for her. Maybe they could even see their mother again. She understood why Billy had had to get away from her – she was always weighing him and measuring him and taking notes on everything that he did and telling him he was rubbish – but secretly, Sally missed her. She was still her mum, after all. (Sally would have been surprised to discover that the mum she missed so much was at that moment lying on her back on the hard cot of her police cell a few blocks away, mentally composing the angry letter to *The Times* that she was going to write about her treatment the moment she was released.)

Sally had made her way from the B&B to the strip of shops close to the waterfront, and now she spotted the newsagent. It was called Thomas's News. It had two displays outside, one of newspapers and one of postcards. Under the postcards were some beach balls in net bags.

Sally went inside. It was a nice place. She liked newsagents, all the shiny-fronted magazines, the brightly wrapped sweets and crisps, and the random things you found in the back, different in every newsagent you went into. This one had lots of colourful exercise books in stacks, and pencils and biros in white plastic tubs. She wondered whether she might be able to get Billy a discount, if they gave her a job here.

Behind the counter was a young man with a shaved head, wearing a checked shirt with the sleeves rolled up. She went over to him.

'Are you Thomas?' she said.

'Yes, well, sort of,' said the man. 'Thomas is my surname, it's a bit annoying having a first name for a surname, people always make that mistake. My first name's Nelson. Which sounds like a surname. Maybe I should have called the place Nelson's.'

'Like the column.'

'Exactly.'

'Well anyway, hello, Nelson. My name's Sally. That's my first name.'

'Sally?' said Nelson. 'Are you Bill's sister?'

'Yes,' said Sally, surprised.

'He was in here earlier, talking about you. He said that you like magazines.'

Sally didn't recall ever having had a conversation with Billy about magazines, but she did like them. Or she didn't not like them.

'Yes,' she said, 'I like magazines.' And, actually, looking around the shop, she could see lots of magazines that she would like to read, given the chance. She hadn't realised there were so many magazines, on so many different subjects. 'I'm here because I'm looking for a job. Do you have any jobs available?'

'I do, actually,' said Nelson. 'We've been busier than I expected and I could do with another pair of hands behind the counter. I can only pay minimum wage I'm afraid, is that OK with you? I'll be able to give you a pay rise, if the place is a success. Fingers crossed.' Nelson smiled.

Sally crossed her fingers and smiled back. This would be a very nice place to work, she decided, especially if Nelson was there all of the time. With his smile, and his checked shirt with the sleeves rolled up.

'That would be fine by me,' she said.

'Great,' said Nelson. 'Come in Monday morning, six o'clock? It's pretty early starts, I'm afraid, working in a newsagent.'

'No problem,' said Sally. 'See you Monday.'

Today was turning out to be a good day.

8.

It occurred to Thandie that eating a full roast lunch with wine was not the best idea just before taking her first yoga class in weeks. Nor, probably, was getting hugely upset, though possibly the yoga might help with that. More likely she would end up sobbing through her sun salutations. She loitered in the lobby of the yoga studio, sipping something called a Karma Revive Soyccino that cost twice as much as a coffee and tasted half as good. Soft music was playing, vaguely oriental instruments wafting over a pulsing beat, occasionally punctuated with whale song. It was doing a great job of making her feel more tense, if that was the intention. She could also have done without the smell of incense in the air, which always reminded her of snogging long-haired poets at university. And look where that had led. She should probably go into the class. If she didn't, she knew it would be several weeks more before she gathered enough willpower to return. But then again, she'd eaten about half of the chicken, even though she'd deliberately left it too long in the oven, out of spite. That chicken was not going to be at all forgiving of her downward-facing dog.

The door from outside opened with, inevitably, the jangling of celestial chimes, and a young man came in, wearing cycling shorts and a loose T-shirt with a picture of the Buddha on it. She observed him for slightly longer than she might have done elsewhere, just because men at the yoga studio were still a rarity, and she was surprised to find him staring back at her. Did she really look so out of place? Yoga wasn't invented by skinny white women, you know! But the man continued to stare. Thandie pretended to pay close attention to her soyccino. Could it be that he was eyeing her up? Surely not. He was very good looking but much younger than her, and probably gay.

Eventually, after a few moments of visible indecision, the man came over to her.

'Excuse me,' he said, 'are you Thandie Evans? Bill's wife?'

Relief washed over Thandie – this was obviously some friend of Bill's, probably an actor. It wasn't particularly unusual to run into people they knew here, as this was the only yoga studio in town.

'Yes, that's me. I'm sorry, I don't recall when we met.' Which was just about the worst thing that you could say to an actor, but after years of tiptoeing around thespian feelings, Thandie no longer cared.

'Oh, it was only once, very briefly,' said the young man. He paused – dramatically, thought Thandie. 'I'm Anthony.' He watched her closely to see her reaction.

'Well, it's nice to meet you again, Anthony.'

Anthony hesitated, seeming to weigh up something in his mind, and then said, 'Would you mind if I had a word with you, in private?'

Thandie glanced up at the clock. Five minutes until the class began. If she started a conversation with this Anthony now, there was no way that she was going to make it. But the kid was looking at her with pleading eyes – argh, I really am a soft touch, she thought.

'Sure,' she said. 'There's a little garden out the back, we can sit there.'

They went outside to a small patio decorated with coloured-glass lanterns and stone statues of Indian gods, and sat at a wrought-iron table that wobbled when Thandie put her soyccino down. A feeling of foreboding began to take hold of her.

Anthony took a breath. 'Bill and I have been, ah, friends, for five months, ever since I was in a production of *A Moment of Madness in May*. I played the spirit who cast the spell on the lovers and made them forget one another. It was a wonderful show.'

There was a note of hopefulness in his voice, that she would remember his performance. Thandie did remember the production, but the actors playing the spirits had all been covered in make-up – she had no specific memory of him on stage. But then it came back to her: Bill introducing his young protégé in the bar after the show, the worshipping way that Anthony had gazed at him, the way Bill's eyes had lingered on Anthony's greasepaint-streaked muscles. Now, as he carried on speaking, she knew, with total conviction, that this man was sleeping with her husband. She felt eerily calm and completely unsurprised. Of course he'd be an actor: the closest Bill could come to shagging one of his own creations.

'I, ah, I ran into Bill, earlier, by chance, totally accidentally, in the pub,' Anthony was saying. 'He was acting very strangely. I mean, *really* strangely. Enough to worry me.'

'He was acting strange at lunch today too,' said Thandie, not at all sure why she was confiding this to her husband's lover.

'He told me that he isn't Bill,' said Anthony. 'That he's literally a completely different person.' He hesitated, then went on, his voice shaking. 'I think he might be having some kind of dissociative episode.'

Thandie almost laughed at the absurdity, but the young man was obviously distressed. She found herself feeling unexpectedly sorry for him. My marriage must truly be dead, she thought. But then she remembered that moment at lunch, Bill wild with indignation at his own treatment of her. It had been sweet, funny, oddly sexy even, and totally out of character. Perhaps what he told Anthony was true, that he did feel like a different person. But maybe this new person was one who was going to return to her? Was that even something that she wanted?

'And he said that he's planning to leave town,' said Anthony. 'Today.'

Or maybe not.

'Could you talk to him?' said Anthony. He looked down at his hands, a red creep of misery spreading up his neck. 'I wouldn't have asked you, but he won't listen to me, and I'm really concerned. As his friend.'

'I'll try and find him,' said Thandie. 'There's no point calling him, his phone got stolen.' She looked over at this poor sad boy, quivering on his ornate wrought-iron chair. 'I'll tell him you were worried,' she added.

9.

When Billy got to the station, there was no sign of Sally, so he waited in a shady spot near the entrance for her to arrive. Before too long, he saw her familiar loping gait, so he waved her over. She greeted him with a huge smile.

'I'm having such a great day!' she said.

'Where's the luggage?' said Billy.

'The luggage?'

'How are we going to leave town without our luggage?'

Sally's face fell. 'Why are we going to leave town? I like it here.'

'I told you. Because there's another Shakespeare.'

'But I just got a job. At the newsagent. Like you told me to.'

Billy felt like a man who, having run headlong into a brick wall, is so disorientated that he runs into the same brick wall again.

'Oh my God,' he said, 'I've been such an idiot. Of course. I should have known. I should have realised.'

'Realised what?' said Sally.

'Have you got enough money for a coffee? I think we should sit down.'

There was a cafe in the station so they went in there. It was over-lit and smelled strongly of yeast, a scent Billy reckoned they piped in to make up for the fact that none of the sweaty-looking pastries on display was baked on site. Sally bought them both things that were advertised as coffees, but which were little more than bitter brown water.

'You know how we weren't made the normal way?' said Billy, pouring something that was approximately milk into his approximately coffee.

'Yes, of course. I'm the control group.'

She sounded proud. Something in Billy's heart broke a little. In order to make her experiment complete, Eleanor had decided that she needed another clone: female to his male, unknown to his known, unexceptional to his exceptional. She had procured a hair from the back of a seat on a number 73 bus for that purpose. Later she would often complain that she hadn't meant for her second clone to be *that* unexceptional. Billy had learned young to notice Eleanor's frustration with Sally before Sally or even Eleanor herself did, and to get Sally out of the way before Eleanor started to vent. Sally still thought she was special, which, of course, she was. But now there was another special Sally.

'You know how we always thought that there was just one of me and one of you?' he said to her. 'Well, it seems like there might be another one of me and another one of you, and they're living in this town.' Billy blinked. Something about this sounded familiar, like déjà vu. Or had he read it somewhere?

Sally meanwhile was nodding.

'Cool,' she said.

'Cool?'

'Yes! Don't you think it's cool? You've got a brother who's exactly like you! And I've got a sister . . .' Sally trailed off. 'Billy, did you talk to Nelson Thomas about me?'

'Who's Nelson Thomas?'

'The man at the newsagent. With the smile. And the nice forearms.'

'No, I haven't been to any newsagent today. How is this relevant?'

'I think I've taken my sister's job. I have to go and tell him!'

'What? No. You don't have to tell anyone anything. In fact, you need to stop interacting with people completely until we can get out of this town.'

'But it isn't fair. Nelson Thomas thinks I'm coming to work on Monday, and he's going to be really pissed off when I don't turn up, and it isn't even really me who isn't turning up, it's my sister.'

'She's not your sister,' said Billy. 'She's another you. Also made from the hair on the bus seat.'

'Like an identical twin.'

'Yes.'

'So she is my sister.'

Billy sighed. 'Yes, if you want to see it that way.' Which meant that William Evans, playwright and poet extraordinaire, husband of the glorious Thandie, was his brother, damn him to hell.

'And I've taken her job.'

'She will survive.'

'I suppose so. Still doesn't seem fair.'

They both sipped their horrible coffees and thought about the implications.

'It was a really nice newsagent,' said Sally.

'So, this morning,' said Billy, 'if it wasn't you who took me to Thandie's house, where were you? Aside from in the newsagent.'

'I got us a B&B, like you asked. And then I took you there.'

'You took me there?'

'Yeah.'

'That wasn't me! You mean you met William Evans?'

'I don't know. I suppose so.'

'Sally! What was he like?'

'He was like you. I don't know! Maybe a bit cleaner? He was talking about his play . . . Oh. So it wasn't you, who wrote the play.'

Shame smacked him in the face like a wave of seawater. 'No,' he snapped, 'it's never bloody me who wrote the play.'

'I'm sure you could write a really good play if you wanted to,' said Sally.

'What do you mean, if I wanted to?'

'Oh, no, I mean, like, when you're ready.'

'You said if I wanted to. Of course I want to.'

'Yeah, of course, I didn't mean anything by it. It's just, you know, when Mum used to make you try, you didn't like it . . .'

'It's who I am, Sally.'

'Yes,' said Sally. 'I know that.'

If he wanted to? Billy was so exasperated that he actually had a mouthful of his coffee. It didn't taste any better now that it was lukewarm.

'So what did he say when you took him to the B&B?' he said.

'Who?'

'William Evans. The other me.'

Sally thought back. 'Thank you? And something about being vegan?'

But if he's vegan, why did Thandie cook him a chicken? This day was getting more confusing all the time.

'So that's why you want to leave?' said Sally. 'Because there's two of each of us, and I've taken her job and he's written your play? But I like it here. Everyone's really friendly. Maybe we can find the other me and the other you and sort it all out with them.'

'It's not you everyone's being friendly towards,' said Billy, 'it's Other Sally. And as for finding them, I don't know about Other Sally, but I don't think that Other Billy is going to be too pleased to see me.'

'Why not?'

'Because right now he might not know that he's actually Shakespeare.'

'Why would that matter?'

'It takes the achievement away, of all the plays and poetry he's written.'

'Does it?' said Sally. 'Why?'

Billy couldn't find a good answer for that.

'The important thing,' he said, 'is that we don't get separated again. Trust me, if the others find out about us, they're going to get very confused and upset. Where did you leave the luggage?'

'At the B&B. With you. I mean with Other Billy.'

'OK. We'll go there together, and I'll wait outside while you get the bags so that Other Billy doesn't see me, and then we'll come back together, and leave, and everything will go back to normal as if none of this ever happened.'

Sally bit her lip. 'What if I don't like normal?' she said.

'Oh, Sally. I'll make it a better normal. I promise. I'll write my own play, and we'll find you another newsagent. But we can't stay here.'

Sally nodded slowly. 'All right. If you say so.' But she didn't sound happy about it.

'Good girl,' said Billy. 'Now, what's the most important thing to remember?'

Sally looked at him blankly.

'Don't get separated,' Billy reminded her.

'Right. Don't get separated.'

At that moment, the door to the cafe opened, and Thandie came in, dressed in exercise gear. Her face was flushed and her hair was awry and to Billy she looked sexier than ever.

'Bill,' she said. 'I thought I might find you here. Anthony . . .' Her voice broke slightly on the name, '. . . told me that you were planning to leave town. You don't have to go. Not because of – him, or anything. Let's just talk about it, OK?'

Billy opened his mouth, then he looked over at Sally.

'Sal,' said Thandie, 'Bill and I really need to talk alone. I tell you what, I'll give you twenty quid and you can go to the pub, yeah?'

Sally raised her eyebrows at Billy.

'Just go to the pub,' he said, 'it'll be fine.'

'But you said—'

'It'll be fine.'

Sally shrugged and took the £20 note Thandie was holding out to her. Then she left the cafe, leaving Billy and Thandie alone.

Thandie sat down in Sally's seat. She turned Sally's cup in its saucer.

'I wouldn't drink that if I were you,' said Billy, 'it's like dishwater.'

'It can't be worse than the Karma Revive Soyccino,' said Thandie, but she didn't take a sip. 'Listen, Bill. I know about Anthony.'

'The traffic warden?'

Thandie was taken aback. 'The actor,' she said. 'Jesus, Bill, how many of them are there?'

'No, no, the actor, of course. He's probably just a traffic warden to pay the bills. That makes sense. Young guy, pale blond hair?'

'Very young,' said Thandie. 'Honestly, Bill, what were you thinking?'

'I have absolutely no idea.'

Thandie leaned back in her chair. 'Look, I didn't come here to fight. I met Anthony, by coincidence, or maybe he was looking for me, I don't know. I'm assuming he doesn't walk around in yoga gear all the time. He seems like a nice lad, and – and very taken with you. I don't want to discuss it, I don't want to know the details. It's just . . . he said that you were acting strangely when he saw you earlier, that you weren't yourself, and you didn't really seem like yourself at lunchtime today either. And the more I think about it, the more I'm worried about you, and – and – he's worried about you too, and we just, both of us, want what's best for you, and for you to be all right.' She leaned forward again across the table, made to touch his hand and then thought better of it.

'Yes,' said Billy slowly, 'I can see that this must be very confusing for you.'

'I actually – and why not be honest now – I actually liked the way you were at lunch today, saying nice things about the house, and that I was a wonderful wife, and . . .' Thandie looked away, out of the window of the cafe. 'Telling me I was beautiful in our wedding photo.'

'You are beautiful,' said Billy. 'Then and now.'

'But – but if you've fallen in love with somebody else – and it doesn't matter that it's a man. Really. That's not the point of what I'm saying. What I'm saying is, I can let you go.' Thandie turned back to him, her eyes brimming with tears. 'The things that Anthony said you told him, that you felt like you weren't yourself any more, that you needed to get away. If it's being stuck with me that's upsetting you that much – it's not worth it, Bill. I don't want you to hurt like that.'

'It's not you,' said Billy. 'Don't say that. None of this is your fault. I'm not in love with Anthony. I'm in love with you.'

Thandie's face filled with hope.

'Do you mean that?' she said.

'As much as I've ever meant anything. Actually, probably more so.'

Now she did take hold of his hand.

'You really are different today,' she said.

Their eyes locked. Billy was filled with the overwhelming desire to kiss her. No, he thought, definitely not. That would absolutely be the wrong thing to do.

But Thandie stood up, pulling him towards her. 'We still need to have a proper conversation about all this,' she said. And then she kissed him.

This is not your wife, Billy reminded himself as he melted into Thandie's delectable embrace. Think of a plan B, there has to be a plan B, a clever plan B that will get me out of this without anybody getting hurt, in just a minute, just one minute, maybe just another minute . . .

10.

Bill waited for Sal to come back. He paced the blue carpet beside the bed – the source of the mushroom smell, he deduced – had a nap to sleep off the whisky he'd had earlier, had a cold shower in the mermaid-themed bathroom down the hall to wash off whatever had rubbed onto him from the sheets (just as well it was a sweltering day, because there was no hot water between 10 a.m. and 6 p.m.), then considered taking another shower to wash off whatever had rubbed onto him from the towel. As time dragged on, and Sal didn't reappear or Anthony answer his text, he began to concede that he might end up having to spend a night here. He reluctantly unpacked, stacking everything in narrow piles as high as possible beside his bag, in order to have minimum contact with the floor – there was nothing as sophisticated as a chest of drawers to put his belongings into. He was intrigued by what Thandie had chosen to pack. Several of his favourite novels – that was surprisingly thoughtful under the circumstances. A somewhat hairy soap. Some jeans and T-shirts, nondescript. Underwear. This gave him pause. It was of a type that he didn't wear. Had

Thandie bought him new underpants? They certainly didn't look new. Did these underpants belong to somebody else – and if so, to whom?

Stranger yet were the notebooks at the bottom of the bag. They were definitely in his handwriting but he didn't recognise the books, nor did he remember having written any of the contents. And he usually made very few corrections as he wrote. These fragments – you couldn't really call them anything else – were heavily crossed out and revised and scrawled over to the point where you could barely read them. Still, there were some original thoughts in there, thoughts he didn't think he'd ever had. He supposed he couldn't remember everything he'd ever thought, what would be the point of having notebooks otherwise? Still, it was uncanny.

Was it possible that he was losing his mind? The memory lapses, that confusion with Sal over when they'd last seen Thandie (perhaps his fault, after all, not hers); these notebooks written, presumably, during manic episodes; the underpants – but no, they definitely weren't his: he couldn't imagine being that insane. It wasn't an entirely unwelcome idea, every writer should experience a bit of madness in his life, and so far it didn't seem that bad; more Hamlet's antic disposition than the full King Lear. (A controversial point amongst scholars, Bill's view being that while Hamlet is certainly faking madness, he begins to lose his grip on the boundary between sanity and insanity, performance and reality. Similar to his own character Herbert, in the play of the same name. King Lear, on the other hand, was plain batshit.)

Still, mad or not, his actions had consequences. Here he was, in a malodorous B&B, contemplating the very real possibility of having to wear another man's underpants. This had all happened very fast. Although in another way, it had been a long time coming. He'd been attracted to Thandie, at first anyway, and he'd loved her, or he'd convinced himself that he did, but deep down what he'd thought was that being in a stable relationship would help support his writing. And then he'd met Anthony – sweet, devoted Anthony – and discovered what love, that is to say love for another human being, really was. Maybe they could get a place together now? Was that rushing things? In any case, though, he owed it to his wife to resolve matters with her first. There was no point phoning her, not the way she'd reacted when he'd tried that this morning, so he decided to go over in person. Maybe he could take a proper shower while he was at it.

He texted Sal quickly to let her know that he was going home to talk to Thandie, and that he'd shout her an ice cream later on the beach. Then he went downstairs, was sent back upstairs by the landlady because he'd left a window open, went downstairs again, tiptoed past reception and then headed across town to his little stone cottage overlooking the sea.

Thandie didn't seem to be home when he let himself in. Both the living room and the kitchen were empty, though on the kitchen counter were the leftovers of the roast lunch she'd cooked for them. He noticed, in the sink, two dirty plates, two sets of cutlery, two glasses with red wine dregs in them. Who had Thandie been having lunch with? The half-empty wine bottle was on the windowsill, and he noticed with some irritation that it was one that his father had given him for a special occasion. Thandie had no business opening it without him.

He grabbed a plastic bag from Thandie's unfathomably huge collection under the kitchen sink and went upstairs with the intention of picking up some of his own blessed underwear. As he approached the bedroom, though, he began to hear the familiar sound of Thandie making love. Or at least, the once-familiar sound. He stopped at the top of the stairs, his mouth dry. He knew that it would be hypocritical of him to be jealous, even though that's exactly what he was. He knew that the best thing he could possibly do right now would be to turn around and leave. He could decide later whether to pretend that he had no idea about it, or to use it against Thandie if she had the gall to complain to him about Anthony. And yet. His wife was just down the hall, making love to another man. How often did an opportunity like this present itself? Not to join in, though to his surprise the image did briefly and, not unpleasantly, pop into his mind. But to witness it, to truly experience the full horror of it, so that he could write about it later.

He crept over to the bedroom door, which had been left ajar. Keeping his breathing as silent as he could, he leaned against the wall, turned and peered through the crack. His wife was on all fours on the bed, facing away from the door, gasping and moaning with every thrust of the interloper, standing behind her. Bill watched the back and forth motion of the man's buttocks, his wife's ecstasy. This is amazing, he thought. So real, so visceral! This is going to make incredible drama! He stood,

68

mesmerised, for what felt like a long time – probably only a few seconds – considered interrupting them, decided against it in case things got violent, then quietly made his way down the corridor again and out of the house, into the sweltering street.

Not knowing what else to do, he headed to the beach. As he walked away from the house, his excitement began to fade, and he became angrier and more self-righteous with every step.

His wife was sleeping with someone else. He'd seen it with his own eyes. Not just sleeping with someone else but very clearly enjoying it. How long had this affair been going on? Was his whole marriage a sham? More of a sham than he thought it was before? Had she even embarked on the affair before he'd started sleeping with Anthony, therefore making the whole thing her fault? Somehow this thought was both appealing and made everything worse.

Reaching the seafront, he pulled off his trainers, let his feet sink into the hot sand, trying to feel something simple and real and good, but it didn't help, and now the sand would get everywhere, like the indignation he was feeling, which was actually a simile that worked much better the other way around, damn it! He gazed out over the waves, picturing, for a moment, walking out into the sea, just walking and walking until he was completely submerged, letting the water fill his lungs, surrendering – *full fathom five thy father lies* – but he dismissed this thought as woefully melodramatic and unworthy of him. Instead, he began to conceptualise a play about an adulterous woman, and the husband who murders her. Not something he'd dream of doing in real life, but there was much to be said for working through your feelings in your writing. The wife accuses the man of infidelity when she's the one at fault? Or maybe it's more interesting if he only thinks that she's been unfaithful . . . He, of course, did not have the luxury of having merely imagined it.

Who was the man who was sleeping with his wife? That's who he should be fantasising about killing, not Thandie, who, he had to admit, had some grounds for the deception. He wished that he'd had the presence of mind to examine the man's discarded underpants, see if they matched the underwear in the suitcase Thandie had packed for him.

Underpants. At a time like this, he's thinking of underpants? What kind of a poet was he?

'Hey, Bill!' called a voice.

It was Sal, coming over the beach towards him – she must have got his message. She waved, and he waved back, faking a smile.

'Are you feeling any better?' she said, as she reached his side.

'Not much.'

'And did you see Thandie?'

Bill was tempted to tell Sal exactly what he'd seen – to enjoy the heat of what would no doubt be her righteous rage on his behalf. At the same time, it would be a humiliating thing to admit. And besides, Sal loved Thandie, and hearing about this would be certain to destroy their relationship. He didn't want to do that to Sal. If he was truly honest with himself, he didn't want to do that to Thandie either. So he just said, 'We didn't talk.'

'I got the tickets,' said Sal.

'What tickets?'

'Out of town.'

'Oh, are you going on a trip?'

'We both are. Aren't we?'

'Not as far as I know.'

Sal's forehead wrinkled as she stared at him, and he could feel his own forehead wrinkling in mirroring confusion.

'You told me to get them,' said Sal.

Bill shook his head slowly, wondering if he could still tell a hawk from a handsaw.

'You did,' said Sal. 'You said, because of the other Shakespeare.'

'What other Shakespeare?'

'I don't know. You said, there's another Shakespeare and we need to leave.'

Try as he might, Bill couldn't remember this conversation or imagine what on earth he might have meant by this.

'You're acting weird again,' said Sal.

'No,' said Bill. The last thing he wanted to do was panic Sal. 'I'm totally fine. There's a completely normal explanation for this. Maybe I wanted you to get tickets for a play? Another Shakespeare play?'

'Oh, yeah, maybe. That would explain why you didn't want me to say goodbye to anybody first.' Sal looked relieved. 'Sorry, I got train tickets. I thought that's what you wanted.'

'That's a shame.' Bill kept his tone light. For all he knew, maybe he had asked her to get train tickets. Maybe he had suggested that she get them first-class flights to Bermuda. 'Well, hopefully they'll take them back. Right, then. Do you want an ice cream?'

'No thanks, I had one earlier. Remember?'

Bill didn't remember. Apparently Bill could no longer remember anything. He needed to talk to someone about this. His dad? But the idea of telling his dad everything that had been going on today chilled him. He'd be so understanding about it, which would only make Bill feel worse. He should probably go to a doctor, even though he hated going to the doctor. First, though, he needed to see Anthony. At least there was no barrier now to the two of them being together. That was one positive thing to come from this whole sordid mess.

'OK, then,' he said. 'I have to, um . . .' Sal didn't know about Anthony, and he didn't want to disappoint her. '. . . go and unpack at the B&B. I'll see you later, yeah?'

'Sure,' said Sal. She was thinking: What B&B?

11.

Sally had a lime and soda in the pub, plus two packets of cheese and onion crisps and some dry roasted peanuts. She had enough money for a burger and fries or the curry of the day, but she wanted to make sure that she saved some of it for Billy. It was his friend who had given it to her after all.

Don't get separated, Billy had said, so she knew she should wait for him in the pub, but time passed and Billy didn't come back, and she was feeling worse and worse about what he had told her about, about her hair-sister. In the end she put what was left of the £20 in her pocket and left the pub, trying not to be tempted back by the tantalising aroma of chicken in a basket being eaten by a grey-haired woman by the door.

Thomas's News was just as she had left it, bar the newspaper display outside being a bit more scant of newspapers. As she pushed the door open and went inside, she noticed, even more than she had before, what a lovely place it was. There were so many little details she hadn't picked up on, like the curlicues around the edge of the 'OPEN / CLOSED' sign on the door, or that the scoop next to the rack of pick and mix was made of polished stainless steel, not plastic, and that the paper bags hanging beside it were all neat and crisp with sharp edges and pink-and-white stripes.

She wondered whether Nelson Thomas would recognise her, she probably hadn't made much of an impression on him, but as soon as she walked in he looked up from the sudoku he was doing and smiled that smile.

'Hello again,' he said. 'I wasn't expecting to see you back until Monday morning.'

'Hello, Nelson,' she said. There was something delicious about his name, even though she didn't feel that she had the right to say it.

'Are you OK?' he said. 'You look a bit down.'

'I'm sorry, but there's been a mistake,' said Sally. She felt so ashamed she couldn't even look him in the eye. 'When I came in earlier, you asked me if I was Billy's sister and I said yes. And that's why you gave me the job. I didn't realise that there was another Sally and another Billy, and that the Billy that you spoke to was the other Billy, and that the Sally you should have given the job to was the other Sally.'

'Well, it's very nice of you to come and tell me that,' said Nelson. 'But I don't know this other Sally. She hasn't been in to see me. You have, and I like you, and I want you to have the job.'

'You like me?' said Sally. She looked up – not as far as his eyes, but as far as his beautiful gleaming forearms.

'Yes,' said Nelson.

74

'Oh.' Sally felt her face go slightly hot, and she hoped that Nelson didn't notice. 'But the thing is, you were never supposed to meet me at all, you were only ever supposed to meet the other Sally. So if you think you like me, maybe it's her that you really like. And it's nice of you to say that I can have the job anyway, but it wouldn't be fair. It's her job. I can't steal it from her. I'm sure she'll come in to see you soon, and then everything will be as it should be.'

'Well, if that's the way you want it,' said Nelson.

'It's not the way that I want it, but it's the way that's right.'

There was a silence. Sally let herself look up a little more, and she saw that Nelson was looking at her, with an expression of quiet admiration. Not that she recognised it as such, being unfamiliar with what an expression of quiet admiration looked like. She knew that it was a good expression though.

'Maybe,' said Nelson, 'you could leave me your phone number, just in case this other Sally doesn't come. Or . . . in case I wanted to call you.'

Now Sally looked him in the eyes. She smiled. He handed her a pad of paper and a pen that were beside the phone on the counter and she wrote down her number and 'Sally' and then in brackets 'the first one'.

'So maybe I'll call you later,' said Nelson.

'Great,' said Sally. She could feel her heart beating hard in a way that she liked.

She was halfway to the door when she turned and added, 'By the way, I should probably mention, the other Sally looks exactly like me. In case that's confusing.'

Nelson frowned.

'We were made from the same hair,' Sally explained. 'OK! Bye then!'

She left the shop feeling happy and excited.

12.

Billy lay in his clone's bed, with his arms around his clone's wife. He found that while he didn't like applying the word to himself, he was more than happy to use it for William Evans. It was hard to pitch the pillow talk precisely. He was in the first flush of something new, while Thandie was basking in the pleasure of a love gone stale, now reignited. Also, she kept saying things like, 'It's like that time in Greece,' to which he could only say, 'Ah yes, Greece.' And then she'd gaze at him with expectation in those huge eyes, and he'd have to come up with something else like, 'Or that time after that thing,' keeping it vague, but who hasn't had a time after a thing? Especially after years of marriage. 'That thing' might even be referring to the wedding itself. But Thandie seemed satisfied. He guessed that she knew exactly which thing he was referring to, even if he didn't.

In a way, he thought, he'd done William Evans a favour. He'd put in a great performance, maybe his best ever, and won Thandie back for him. It was selfless, actually. He was sure William Evans would see it that way.

But as for Thandie ... Billy felt the stirrings of guilt in his stomach, a feeling he disliked intensely. He told himself that he had nothing to reproach himself for. He hadn't meant to lie to Thandie. She'd been lied to enough, in his opinion. And if telling the truth had ever been an option, it wasn't any more. Thandie was happy. She was radiant with it. She thought her husband loved her. What possible purpose would it serve to take that happiness away from her? Billy wondered what it would be like to be able to make a woman that happy for real. It must be the most wonderful feeling in the world. Anyway, lying about sleeping with someone behind your wife's back is totally different from lying about being a secret Shakespeare clone who has been accidentally, and through no fault of his own, forced into impersonating the person-you-are-lying-to's husband. His conscience could almost entirely be clear.

It was bliss to lie in this soft, comfortable bed – no sunken mattresses or broken springs poking into his back – with Thandie in his arms. He wished he could stay there forever. But given that that was impossible, it did make sense to treat this moment as an information-gathering opportunity. But how? The questions that presented themselves weren't exactly ones that he could ask directly. For example:

- Does William Evans know that he is a clone of Shakespeare?
- Even if he does know, do you, Thandie, know it?
- Who is William Evans's – and, by extension, my – father?

- Why weren't we raised together?
- Why does William Evans have everything while I, William Anderson, have nothing?

Why do I have nothing? He felt the self-pity welling up, a feeling he far preferred to guilt. He snuggled in behind Thandie so that she could no longer see his face, his body fitting perfectly against hers – another, less pressing question could not stop itself from breaking through, which was what did they call spooning before the invention of spoons? – and he buried his face in her sweet-smelling neck.

'How well do you think you know me?' he asked her.

There was a long silence. Maybe he should have asked the question about the spoons. Then Thandie said, 'If you'd asked me that yesterday, I would have said that I know you very well. Maybe even better than you know yourself. But today . . .' She shook her head, her hair tickling his cheek. 'It's like you're transformed. The way you've been looking at me. Like you actually really see me, for the first time in years. I don't know. My friends would think I'm mad, welcoming you back in my bed after . . .' There were obviously words that she didn't want to say. 'But you're my husband. We've got work to do. But you're still my husband.'

'I am indeed your husband.' And we'll remain happily married as long as you never allude to this encounter ever having taken place.

Billy planted a row of kisses along Thandie's shoulder blade. 'Do you ever wonder if I would have turned out differently if I had been raised by my mother instead of my father?' he said. This question was a risk. For all he knew, William Evans's father had installed a fake mother – perhaps someone with more natural warmth than the icy Eleanor Anderson.

'That's one of those unanswerable questions,' said Thandie. 'Did you ever get a reply from that email you sent her?'

'The . . . email . . .'

'I would have thought she'd want to meet you,' continued Thandie. 'That she'd have some curiosity about you at least.'

'Yes,' said Billy. 'I certainly would have thought that as well.'

'Do you think . . .' Thandie shifted a bit, causing her buttocks to graze his penis in an agonisingly delicious way. 'Do you think that's why you've been acting so strangely? All that dissociative stuff, the actor, um . . .' She stopped, back in the danger zone. 'And being so affectionate today. Are you having some kind of belated reaction to her abandonment of you? I still think maybe you should go and talk to somebody about it.'

'Maybe,' said Billy, 'being abandoned by my mother is what makes me a writer. Unless you can think of any other reason that I might have become a writer. Any reason.'

'Who can say why anyone becomes anything?' said Thandie. 'I've always found it surprising that, with both of your parents having a science background, neither you nor Sal have ever shown any interest in science at all.'

'Yes, that is surprising.'

Billy tried to formulate a casual-sounding question about whether his scientific father had any interest in human cloning, but there is no casual-sounding question about human cloning, so he reluctantly abandoned that line of investigation.

He thought for a little longer. He stroked Thandie's breasts while he thought, seeing as they were there. 'Do you like my dad?' he asked.

'It's a bit weird to be thinking about your dad while you're doing that.'

With regret, Billy stopped moving his hand. 'But do you?'

'Of course. Everybody likes your dad.'

'And nobody likes my mum.'

As soon as the words were out of his mouth, Billy could have kicked himself, but Thandie said, 'Well, that's what he always says, but maybe he's just bitter.'

'Maybe.' But probably not. Billy thought back to the last time he had seen Eleanor. It was her birthday and he'd got them tickets to see *Hamlet*. Billy would have preferred to have hated Shakespeare, but he had to settle for resenting him, because whenever he saw one of the plays, read one of the poems, his soul would come alive. *Hamlet* was Shakespeare's masterpiece, in Billy's opinion, and he thought that, in this case, his opinion counted for more than most. Every character in *Hamlet* is living their own tragedy. It could just as easily have been called Gertrude, Cordelia, Claudius, Laertes. Just like life, Billy thought. Life has no protagonist. For once, he was curious, truly curious, about Eleanor, about why she had done it.

After the show – terrible staging; it was impossible to ruin *Hamlet*, but goodness knows, directors kept trying – Billy had queued for almost half an hour in the theatre bar to buy two glasses of overpriced, sour white wine that at least had the dignity to be bitingly cold. Back at the table, he'd sat down opposite the mother with whom he had nothing in common except that they were both players in this bizarre game.

'Puerile production,' said Eleanor.

Broadly speaking Billy agreed, so maybe they had one thing in common, but he wasn't going to give her the satisfaction of saying so.

'Tell me something,' he said instead, 'was it worth it?'

'Sitting through three and a half hours of that?' said Eleanor.

'The experiment. Making us. Was it worth it?'

'Billy,' said Eleanor, 'one of the things that has never ceased to amaze me in all of these years is your almost total lack of vision. I have never met anybody less capable of looking beyond the accumulation of fluff in his own belly button. You want to know if it was worth it?' She leaned towards him, lowering her voice to a hiss. 'I made a human clone, and not just any clone. I could have cloned myself, that's what a lesser scientist, a vainer scientist would have done. I cloned William Shakespeare, the greatest writer, possibly the greatest thinker the world has ever seen. I wasn't content with the immense complexity of perfecting the science of human replication. I wasn't content with exploring the conundrum of nature versus nurture. I attempted nothing less than to summon the presence of purest genius, to make lightning strike twice, to study it, to learn from it, to give it to the world. And I ended up with you. Was it worth it?' She sat back in her seat. 'Of course it wasn't worth it. It's obvious that whoever William Shakespeare was, he didn't write the *Complete Works of Shakespeare*. I suppose I'll have to go through the same rigmarole with the Earl of Oxford.'

Billy's hand tightened on his plastic cup of wine.

'And Sally?' he said.

'Oh, Sally. If you'd ever bothered to read Virginia Woolf, you'd be familiar with her question: What would have happened had Shakespeare had a sister? I dreamed I could come up with an answer. Woolf, of course, was imagining an incredibly gifted young woman, but, ever the scientist, I made the mistake of being too preoccupied with creating an ideal contrast to you, or what I thought you'd be, anyway. I shouldn't have gone to the trouble. Sally was a waste of a test tube.'

Billy stood up and left without another word. The next day, he and Sally packed up everything they owned, got in his old Ford Fiesta – this was long before the Fiesta broke down for the last time on a B road just outside Glasgow – and drove to Liverpool. Billy didn't know why he'd chosen Liverpool, but it had certain associations for him: a port, a place of coming and going, a place of creativity. They'd stayed two months before Billy decided that the pressure of trying to write in the home of the Beatles was too much for him. He may be William Shakespeare but he was no John Lennon.

In the moment that he'd left the theatre bar, he'd felt a sense of triumph, of rejecting everything his mother stood for, of buying into her actions so little that he wasn't even going to show her that he cared enough to want answers, real answers, not just her sarcastic dismissal. Now he wished that he'd got those answers while he had the chance. Maybe he wouldn't have wandered so long if he wasn't looking for himself. Of course, he had no idea that he would literally find himself, and that he'd be living in a seaside town with a beautiful wife and a successful writing career. And a young traffic warden/actor for a boyfriend . . . Clearly, William Evans did not have all the answers either.

'Would you say we've been happy in our marriage?' Billy asked Thandie now.

Thandie rolled over onto her back and stared up at the ceiling. After a while, she said, 'No.'

'So why did we get married?'

'Because we love each other. Or at least we did. But love and happiness are not the same thing. And you love your work more than you ever loved me. Nothing fulfils you the way that writing does. I come a very distant second.'

'That can't be true.'

'Come on, Bill! You know it better than I do.'

'I mean, I'm compelled to write, obviously. But surely no writer actually enjoys it?'

'It's everything to you! It's so much a part of you, I can't even imagine who you'd be without it. You'd be miserable, wouldn't you? Always feeling like there was something missing, that you weren't complete. You'd be pretty unbearable to be around.'

'You really do know me very well,' said Billy.

He took one last look at Thandie, the curling black hair, the sensual mouth, the soft, rounded body that had so recently bent and touched and held and opened to him. He knew he had fallen in love with her, and therefore that he had to get as far away from her as possible.

'I need to go find Sally . . . Sal,' he said. 'We sent her off to the pub ages ago, she'll be wondering where I am.'

'Why don't you call her . . . oh, yeah, I forgot, your phone was nicked. You can use mine if you like.'

'No, I need to talk to her in person. She's, ah, really upset about being out of work.'

'Oh, of course. Give her a hug from me. Will you be home for dinner?'

Home, thought Billy.

'I don't think so,' he said. He leaned over and brushed a lock of hair away from Thandie's forehead. 'I'm sorry for everything. I really mean that. You're far too good for me.'

Billy didn't know whether he was speaking for William Evans or for himself.

13.

Sal was so frustrated she was close to tears. The woman at the counter was refusing to take the tickets back, even though Sal had only just bought them, and had explained to her that it was all a misunderstanding with her brother.

'But we're not going to use them,' said Sal. 'We won't be on the train. Other people can sit in our seats.'

'The tickets are non-refundable,' the woman said again.

'Yes,' said Sal, 'you've said that. Quite a few times. But I don't understand why you can't give us our money back when we're not going to use the tickets. It's not like when you buy a dress and you change your mind and try to take it back, but you've already worn it and it smells a bit of armpits. We're not going to travel so we shouldn't have to pay.'

'The tickets are non-refundable.'

The woman, Sal thought, looked like she might smell a bit of armpits, but she didn't know for sure, because she was sitting behind a plastic screen with only a little slot underneath to pass money and tickets back and forth.

'Can we swap them for different tickets to somewhere else? Or to the same place on a different day?'

'The tickets are non-exchangeable,' said the woman.

'What's going on? Did you buy the tickets already?' Sal turned. It was Bill (or she had no reason to believe it was anybody other than Bill).

'Yes, I told you,' said Sal, 'but I got train tickets instead of theatre tickets, so I was trying to give them back except this lady won't take them.'

'The tickets are non-refundable,' said the woman.

'We don't need to give them back. I just messaged you that we need to leave right away. Don't you ever check your phone?'

Sal pulled her phone out of her pocket to check for messages. Billy stared at it for a moment.

'Is that your phone?' he said. 'Your phone is blue?'

'Yes. I don't have any messages from you, though.'

'Um ... that would be right,' said Billy. 'Because I didn't send you any.'

'But you just said that you just messaged me.'

'Yes. I was confusing you with someone else.'

Sal began to feel worried. Bill might insist that he hadn't been acting weird, but he was definitely acting weird, and she didn't know what to do about it.

'How could you confuse me with someone else?' she said. 'I'm your sister.'

'I ... ah ... it's complicated.'

'Are you two planning on buying any tickets?' said the woman behind the counter. 'Because people are waiting.'

Sal and Billy glanced behind them. An old man in full hiking gear was standing there.

'That's not people,' said Billy. 'That's one person.'

'Bill . . .' said Sal.

'I'm waiting too,' said the woman. 'I'm waiting for you to make up your mind. So him and me together, we're people.'

'You're in customer service and I'm a customer,' said Billy.

'You're only a customer if you buy something.'

'My train's in five minutes,' said the man in the hiking gear.

'Bill, let's get out of the way,' said Sal. She turned to the woman behind the counter. 'I'm sorry about my brother, he's not very well at the moment.'

'That's not really my problem,' said the woman.

'I'm completely fine,' said Billy.

'Four minutes,' said the man in the hiking gear.

'Bill,' said Sal firmly. 'Let's go and stand over there.'

She guided her brother to one side.

'Bill,' she said. 'I'm worried about you. First, you said that you wanted to leave town, then you said that you didn't want to leave town. And when I said what you said, you said you never said that you wanted to leave town.' Sal paused for a moment to count up the number of times she'd said *said* to make sure that she'd got it right. 'Yes. And now you're here and you're saying that you want to leave town again. And that you're confusing me with someone else. Who are you confusing me with, Bill?'

Billy didn't say anything for a few moments. Sal started to feel dizzy: Bill was supposed to be the sensible one, the clever one, the one who always knew what to do. Finally, he sighed.

'Sal,' he said. 'That is your name, right?'

'You're scaring me, Bill,' said Sal.

'I'm sorry,' said Billy. 'I'm not trying to scare you. It's just a strange situation, probably stranger than anything you've ever experienced before. Listen to me very carefully, Sal. Your brother Bill and I are . . .' He flinched slightly, then continued, '. . . clones, which is basically the same thing as identical twins. And you've got a clone as well. That's who I was confusing you with. For some reason I don't know, you and your brother were raised by your father, and me and my sister were raised by our mother.'

'My sister and I,' said the man in the hiking gear.

'Go and catch your train!' yelled Billy.

The man scuttled away to the platform.

'It was a complete coincidence that we happened to come here to this town today,' Billy continued. 'I want you to know that. And now that we've realised how complicated things have got, we're going to leave, and everything will go back to normal for you. But I know you're going to end up telling Thandie all about this, so the important thing to remember when you do that is to tell her that I love her. OK? Don't forget that. Tell Thandie I love her. There is only one Thandie.'

Sal nodded slowly. Bill was right. Thandie was the one reliable constant. 'I need to go to the loo,' she said. 'I'll be back in a minute. Don't go anywhere.'

'I'm not going to go anywhere,' said Billy.

'Don't sell him any train tickets!' Sal said to the woman behind the counter.

'I'm mandated to serve where service is required.'

She definitely smelled of armpits, thought Sal, as she made her way into the ladies' loos. Armpits and bums.

Once the door of the ladies' was closed behind her, Sal quickly dialled Thandie's number.

'Thandie,' she said when her sister-in-law picked up, 'it's an emergency. I'm at the station and Bill is here. He's acting really crazy.' Sal started to cry.

'It's OK, Sal, it's OK,' said Thandie. 'I've just seen him, he's fine.'

'No,' said Sal, 'he isn't. He's saying all these mad things about being a clone and that I'm a clone as well. And he says he wants to leave town straight away and he just told me to tell you that he loves you. I don't think he's planning to come back! You have to come and stop him.'

There was a pause. Then Thandie, sounding tired and sad, said, 'OK, Sal, I'm on my way. Try not to let him leave.'

'I'm not a clone, Thandie!' said Sal.

'No, sweetie,' said Thandie, 'you're not. Don't worry. You're not a clone.'

14.

Bill tried to call Anthony three times on the way over to his place, but Anthony didn't pick up. He'd never been to his place before. Anthony was only twenty and still lived with his mum and dad, and while they knew he was gay, he said that they wouldn't approve of him being in a relationship with a man more than ten years older than him, especially one who was married. Bill had never met them. When he walked Anthony home, they'd say goodbye around the corner, and then he'd watch Anthony walk away, feeling agreeably heartbroken each time, as well as appreciative of Anthony's great backside.

Bill rang the doorbell, running through plausible cover stories in his head, should one of Anthony's parents answer the door. Simply saying he was a 'friend of Anthony', he feared, would reveal too much, as well as be far too boring. He was a fellow traffic warden, wanting to swap shifts. He was a local business owner to whom Anthony owed money. He was an angry driver, here for revenge over an unfair parking ticket. Bill was almost disappointed when the door opened and Anthony himself was on the other side, now out of his uniform and looking adorably tousled in shorts and a strikingly ugly Buddha T-shirt. He was, however, stony-faced.

'I'd thought you'd get the message when I didn't pick up,' said Anthony. 'Obviously not.'

'Why? What's the matter? Are your parents at home?'

'No. Just me. Mum'll be back from work soon, though.'

'So, can I come in? If I'm still here when your mum gets back, we can tell her I'm a Jehovah's Witness.'

'She'll never believe that. You're wearing shorts. Jehovah's Witnesses never show their knees.'

But Anthony led the way into the flat all the same.

'I thought someone nicked your phone, anyway,' he said.

'What made you think that?' Bill asked.

Anthony didn't reply. Yet another thing Bill couldn't remember. But he definitely still had his phone. He gripped it in his hand like a talisman.

It was even hotter inside than it was out of doors, and the flat was decorated in bright, clashing colours that seemed to pulsate in the heat. It reminded Bill of something, but he couldn't quite think what.

'Is there maybe a garden or a patio, or something? Somewhere cooler and more . . . monochrome? Where we can talk?'

'Nope,' said Anthony. He took Bill into an open-plan kitchen–living room. The walls were purple, the curtains were yellow, and the kitchen tiles were designed to look like sweets. The whole place throbbed like a migraine. It occurred to Bill that it might be even easier to persuade Anthony to move in with him than he had thought. Not that Anthony was looking particularly amenable to persuasion right now, perched on the edge of a pink armchair and refusing to sink back into the cushions. Bill settled on a green sofa opposite him.

'Is everything all right?' Bill said. 'You seem a little furious.'

'I see you haven't left town – yet,' said Anthony.

'I've got no intention of leaving town.' Bill thought of his conversation with Sal, her insistence that he had told her to buy train tickets. Once again the threads of reality seemed to be slipping from his fingers. 'Did I tell you that I was leaving town?'

'Yes. You did. Or wait, it wasn't "you". You were very clear about that. You said that you were a completely different person.'

My God, thought Bill, maybe I have multiple personality disorder?

'I'm sorry,' he said. 'I don't remember . . .'

'At first, I was worried about you,' said Anthony. 'I was so worried that I spoke to Thandie—'

'You spoke to my wife?'

'—And she said that you had seemed strange to her too, at lunch—'

'But I didn't have lunch with Thandie—'

'—And it was only later that I really thought back over it, over what you said, that you don't love me, you don't want to be with me, you're leaving and never coming back, so, yeah, excuse me if I'm, what's the word you used? Furious.'

Multiple personality disorder for sure! How prescient of his other personality to have kept notebooks – he could hardly wait to get back to the B&B and read them properly. Or he supposed it could be early-onset Alzheimer's. He really hoped not, although that would be fascinating to write about, if you caught it right on the cusp. Or you could have an older character who at the start still seems lucid, with maybe signs of bad judgement, nothing more, and gradually follow his descent. Actually, it would be interesting to do it from the point of view of his family, and whether they support him or abuse his vulnerability, and maybe he trusts the wrong ones – and is that because of the disease, or is it just that he's always been too blind to see what they are doing to him – wait, had this already been done . . .

'Bill,' said Anthony. 'Are you listening?'

'I'm sorry,' said Bill. 'I don't remember any of this. And even if I did say those things, I promise you, I didn't mean them. Or this personality didn't mean them . . . You know, I think I should probably go and see a doctor.'

'Yes, I think you should.' A shard of concern cracked through Anthony's angry demeanour.

'Wait, though. First . . .' Bill leapt forward and took Anthony's hand. Because he'd emerged from the squishiness of the green sofa, he landed awkwardly on his knee, which gave his back a twinge, and also, he realised, put him into the classic proposal position, which was not what he wanted at all, although, maybe, one day? Marriage, kids – a man as beautiful as Anthony should have loads of kids. But first, hauling himself to his feet, the question he'd meant to ask, not so romantic sounding, but crucial nonetheless: 'Will you move in with me?'

'Really?' said Anthony. Bill couldn't help but notice him glance at the yellow curtains which, he now observed, were covered in a pattern of seashells in a contrasting peach.

Just then they heard the turn of the key in the lock of the front door.

'My mum!' said Anthony.

'If we're going to move in together,' said Bill, keeping hold of Anthony's hand, 'you're going to have to tell her about us. So why not do it now?'

'You home, love?' called Anthony's mother.

'Come on,' said Bill. 'I love you. It's time.'

They were still holding hands when Anthony's mother walked into the room. She stopped, confused, taking in the scene.

'The vegan,' she said.

'The eccentric landlady!' said Bill.

'You know each other?' said Anthony.

'He's staying at Shady Palms,' said Violet. 'Checked in today.'

'Is that right?' Anthony asked Bill.

'Sal booked the room after Thandie . . .' Too late, Bill realised the implications of what he was saying.

'Found out about me and threw you out,' Anthony finished the sentence. 'And now suddenly you want to move in together. What a coincidence.'

'It's not like that,' said Bill. 'And I thought you said your mother was a hotelier?'

'She is!'

'I was imagining . . .' . . . something a lot more salubrious than Shady Palms. From the look on Violet's face, Bill needed to stop starting sentences that it was so easy for other people to finish.

'Move in? With that old creep?' said Violet.

'Don't worry, Mum,' said Anthony, dropping Bill's hand. 'It's not going to happen.'

'I never imagined you with a vegan,' said Violet.

'That was actually a misunderstanding about a chair,' said Bill.

'I think you should go,' said Anthony.

'I'm not giving up on you,' said Bill.

'But I'm giving up on you.'

Anthony turned away.

'Anthony – please . . .'

'Just go.'

Violet was tapping her foot. It made soft whumping sounds on the shaggy turquoise carpet. Bill realised, reluctantly, that no matter what he had just said, he was going to have to give up on this battle, though not, he swore to himself, the war.

Violet escorted him out. 'See you tomorrow morning,' she said. 'There's a continental breakfast buffet from seven 'til nine, only one mini-cereal box per guest, and the milk's UHT but you won't be needing that.'

She shut the door behind him, leaving him alone in the street. Suddenly being mad didn't seem quite so fascinating any more. With a sinking heart, Bill decided that he had to talk to a doctor. As if this day could get any worse.

With any luck I'll forget this ever happened, he thought. He didn't think he could ever forget Anthony, though.

15.

The doctor's office was still open when Bill arrived. Bill had never liked going to the doctor, ever since he was a child. The worst part was the waiting room. He would look at all the other patients and wonder what was wrong with them, and whether it was contagious. Then he would look at all the surfaces and think of all the bacteria and viruses multiplying on each one. The supposedly helpful posters on the walls detailing the warning signs of stroke and recommending flu jabs only served to make everything worse. This was the downside to having an imagination.

Today he did his best to ignore the mothers with their sticky-fingered children spreading their germs everywhere, and the elderly people with their, he assumed, weeping sores, and made his way to the reception desk.

'Do you have an appointment?' asked the receptionist. Bill didn't recognise him, he must be new. He was a youngish man with a large neck tattoo.

'No,' said Bill, 'but it's an emergency.'

'What kind of emergency?'

'I'm mad.'

'OK,' said the receptionist, 'and how long have you been mad for?'

'Just since today.'

'Right. Well, I'll put you on the list. Take a seat.'

Bill scanned the seats and tried to figure out which one would have had the least exposure to other human beings, and sat on that one. There were piles of old magazines to read, but he resolved not to touch any of them. They were a contamination hot-spot. He wondered whether anybody had ever done a study of disease transmission rates from magazines found in doctors' surgery waiting rooms. He got out his phone and googled it. They had. The results were not encouraging. Then he googled whether anybody had ever done a study of disease transmission rates from mobile phones. They had. The results were even worse. Soon he had fallen down a black hole of disease transmission studies from everyday objects and situations and was making a mental list of things to avoid in his future life (door handles, children, seat-back tables on aeroplanes, shaking hands, bean sprouts) when his name was called.

'Ah, Bill,' said the doctor, closing the examination room door behind him.

'Dr Patel,' said Bill.

Dr Patel held out his hand for Bill to shake. Bill looked at the hand, and at the door handle. 'Would you mind if I didn't shake your hand?' he said. 'Nothing personal.'

'Of course,' said Dr Patel, as if this happened all the time. 'Please, sit. Unless you would prefer to stand?'

Bill considered the likelihood of the chair being toxic, before resolving that even if it were, he would be unlikely to catch anything by having it touch the backs of his thighs. Christ, he thought, I really am losing it. He crossed everything off his previous mental list of things to avoid and replaced them with one word: googling. Then he sat down.

Dr Patel also sat down, behind his desk. An electric fan on the desk slowly moved back and forth, blowing cool air at Dr Patel, then at him, then at Dr Patel, then at him.

'So what can I help you with today?' said Dr Patel. 'I understand that you are . . .' He glanced at his computer screen. 'Mad.'

'Yes, that's right,' said Bill.

'And you've been mad for one day?'

'That's right,' said Bill again.

'And how has this "madness" manifested itself?'

'I think I might be having blackouts. People keep telling me that I've said things or done things or been places that I haven't said or done or been.'

'What kind of things?'

'Things like . . . that I saw them earlier on, when I know I didn't, or that I told them to buy train tickets.' It sounded puny, said out loud.

'I see,' said Dr Patel. 'And this has only been occurring today?'

'Yes.'

'Are you under any particular stress at the moment?'

'Yes. Yes, I am.' Bill took a deep and, he hoped, not germ-saturated breath. 'Can I count on your discretion?'

'Of course. Anything you say to me here is entirely confidential.'

'Dr Patel. As you know, I am a married man, but the truth is that I also have – or had – a lover. And today both my wife and my lover have left me.'

Dr Patel looked momentarily shocked, but swiftly concealed it. Bill knew it had been a mistake to come to his regular surgery. Still, it was too late now. All he could do was try to get the sympathy back to his side.

'I caught Thandie in bed with another man,' he said. 'She kicked me out.' True, it hadn't happened in that order, but he couldn't help but give in to his instinct for drama. 'My lover rejected me when I went to him for help. Yes! "Him"! And now I have to live in a B&B where the landlady is my ex-lover's mother. The B&B is filthy, by the way.'

Dr Patel nodded. 'That does sound like a stressful day.'

'It is!' Tears sprung to Bill's eyes – was he turning into one of those men who cried a lot? Was that a symptom of his infirmity?

'Have you taken any drugs today?' asked Dr Patel.

'No,' said Bill. 'I never take drugs. Although I did have a whisky and ginger earlier. Around lunchtime.'

'At lunchtime? And what did you have for lunch?'

Bill tried to remember. Nothing came to mind. 'I can't remember,' he said. 'Sal said that I had lunch with Thandie, but I don't think I did. You see? This is what I mean! In fact, I think I might have forgotten to have lunch. I'm really hungry.'

Dr Patel nodded again. 'Are you accustomed to drinking at lunchtime?'

'No, not really. Well, sometimes. Yes.'

Dr Patel typed something into his computer.

'Have you been experiencing any delusions?' he asked.

'Not as far as I know.'

'Hearing voices?'

'No.'

'Feelings of grandiosity?'

Bill hesitated. Then he said: 'Sometimes I think I am a truly great writer. I mean, Shakespeare-great.'

'I'll put that down as a "maybe",' said Dr Patel. 'Have you had any thoughts of harming yourself or other people?'

'No.'

'Have you been having any symptoms at all aside from these lapses in memory?'

'No. Unless you count getting really freaked out about all the germs in your waiting room.' Bill was beginning to feel slightly foolish. He found himself wanting to convince Dr Patel that he was mad, rather than that he wasn't.

'I don't count that,' said Dr Patel. 'It's not entirely irrational. Indeed, I would advise all patients wash their hands before they arrive and after they leave. It's a basic precaution. I wash my own hands between every patient, of course.'

This seemed slightly pointed. 'I can shake your hand now, if you really want me to,' said Bill.

'That won't be necessary.'

'So . . .' said Bill. 'Am I mad?'

'Mr Evans, "mad" is not a clinical term. It's really a layman's expression for a range of mental health conditions, perhaps encompassing schizo-affective disorder, schizophrenia, psychosis and so on. None of which describes you. It is my professional opinion that you are suffering from low blood sugar combined with extreme stress, possibly exacerbated by dehydration due to the unusually warm weather conditions today. You appear to have some issues with health anxiety, perhaps generalised anxiety too, and you might want to give some thought to your drinking habits. I suggest that you return to your bed and breakfast, have a sandwich and a drink – no alcohol – and get an early night. If your symptoms continue to bother you, do by all means make another appointment to see me, and we can consider whether a course of antidepressants or CBT might be of use. For now, try to relax. Maybe do some yoga. And don't forget to wash your hands after you leave.'

'We're not allowed to eat at the B&B,' said Bill, feeling peculiarly disappointed.

'I'm sure that you will be able to work your way around that particular difficulty without my guidance,' said Dr Patel. 'Have a pleasant weekend.'

16.

Billy paced back and forth, ignoring the theatrical sighs of the woman behind the ticket counter. So close to leaving without a trace! Well, Bill and Sal and Thandie would have pieced something together themselves, some kind of story to explain it all. The fact that this story would now be the truth was regrettable, but probably the best of a number of bad options. At least by the time Thandie found out he'd lied to her (a white lie, under terrible duress), he'd be long gone.

Sal was still in the ladies' – why did women always take so long in the loo? – so Billy called Sally, but she didn't pick up.

Billy texted her: 'Where are you? We need to go.'

But Sally didn't text back.

Billy sent another text: 'I'm waiting for you at the station. HURRY.' He was about to add, 'I'm here with Other Sally', but at that moment Other Sally came out of the loo, and so Billy quickly pressed 'send' and put the phone back in his pocket.

'I'm hungry,' said Sal. 'Shall we get something from the cafe?'

Billy never turned down food, particularly when someone else was buying, so he went into the cafe with Sal.

'I don't have any money on me,' he told her.

'That's OK,' said Sal.

'And also, I'm not your brother. It's important that you don't buy this Danish pastry for your brother, William Evans. You should only buy it for me, William Anderson. And also a latte. Double shot.'

'Yes, Bill,' said Sal.

She bought the coffee and the Danish pastry, and a packet of cheese and onion crisps for herself. Billy noticed her checking out the magazine display, but apparently she didn't see anything she liked the look of, because she sat down without picking any of them up. There were several celebrity magazines at the front, the type where a circle is drawn around the fat bit poking out of the top of a reality star's bikini, and Billy wondered, not for the first time, what would happen if it got into the press that he – and Bill – were reproductions of Shakespeare. Would there be long lens photos of them hanging out on yachts? Not that Billy had ever been on a yacht. Quite aside from anything, he suffered from seasickness.

Sal picked out a table and sat down, and Billy joined her.

'I know that you don't believe me,' he said, 'but in a minute the other Sally – my sister Sally – is going to arrive, and I don't want you getting too upset.' Where the hell was Sally? Billy took his phone out of his pocket, in case he hadn't noticed a message come through, but all there was was a banner alert from some app telling him that he hadn't done a crossword in a while. 'I probably shouldn't have told you the truth at all, but I've tried lying and I've tried telling the truth. And they're both rubbish.'

Sal opened her bag of crisps. Billy noticed that she ate her crisps the same way Sally did, looking for the biggest ones in the bag first and trying to fit them whole into her mouth without breaking them.

'You're eating the big ones first,' he said.

'Yes,' said Sal. 'They taste better than the broken bits. I don't know why. And they're more fun to eat.'

Which was exactly what Sally had said, when he'd asked her about it.

'Tell me something,' he said to her. 'What's Bill like?'

Sal didn't like this question. He saw her chin begin to wobble.

'Humour me,' he said. 'Pretend that I'm not Bill.'

Sal steadied herself. She put her packet of crisps down. Billy wondered whether he could have one – the Danish was far too sweet, and he could do with something salty to cut through it – but he decided that asking her right now wouldn't be a good idea.

'Fine,' Sal said. 'If you want to know, Bill is the best big brother in the world. He's always looking out for me and making sure I'm OK. The thought that something bad might have happened to him really scares me. I just want him to be OK and to be my big brother again.'

Something in Billy's chest lurched. She reminded him so much of Sally, not only in the obvious ways, but she was the same sweet, trusting, naive kind of girl that he had always tried, in his own imperfect way, to do his best by. Or at least he thought he had. He asked himself how much better his best might be, if he actually put a bit of effort into it.

'Oh, Sal,' he said. 'I'm sorry. I didn't mean to frighten you.' He thought of saying: Of course, it's me, it's Bill, your brother. Everything is fine. But Sally might arrive at any moment. (Where in God's name was she?) And then how would he explain?

'But you are frightening me, Bill,' said Sal.

Billy looked out of the window of the cafe, hoping to see Sally and their luggage approaching so that he could put an end to all this, but instead he saw a car pulling up in the station car park and Thandie getting out. He watched as she put money into the pay-and-display machine and wondered whether there was any way that he could jump up now and start running. But where would he go? Besides, if it was a choice between being in the same room with Thandie again and not being in the same room with Thandie again, he was going to choose being in the same room as her, regardless of the fact that he was doing everything he could to get away from her. There was no logic to that, but it made sense to him all the same.

He lost sight of Thandie for a few seconds as she made her way round to the entrance to the cafe, soon to appear again, like the sun from behind a cloud, he thought, a totally clichéd image that Shakespeare would never use – though actually,

Billy remembered, he did, in *Henry IV Part 1*, Act 1, Scene 2. And in 'Sonnet 33'. Ha! What a hack.

'Did you call Thandie?' he said to Sal. 'Did you tell her what I said?'

'I thought she'd know what to do,' said Sal.

Thandie hurried into the cafe and breathlessly made her way to their table.

'I've been so stupid,' she said. 'You're not yourself. I should have known.'

Billy's heart leapt. 'So you believe me? I mean, what Sal told you?'

'Come with me,' said Thandie. 'I've got the car. We'll talk.'

'This is amazing. You're not angry?'

'No, of course I'm not angry.'

'Even though I let you think I was Bill? When we – you know? I never planned to, but you can see why I didn't think I could tell you the truth.'

'Have you paid?' Thandie asked Sal. Sal nodded.

The three of them walked to the car together and got in, Billy in the front with Thandie, Sal behind.

'All my life I've kept this secret,' Billy was saying. 'My mother always said that I should never tell anybody.'

'Your . . . mother?' said Thandie.

'Yes – she said that if anybody found out she'd go to jail. Human cloning is illegal, you see. Can you imagine, all through school, knowing who I was and not being able to tell any of my friends, my teachers, anyone?'

They were moving now. 'What do you mean, knowing who you were?' said Thandie.

'Oh, of course, I didn't tell Sal that part. Bill and I aren't just any old clones. We're clones of Shakespeare.'

'Shakespeare.' Thandie didn't sound very excited about that. Maybe she wasn't surprised?

'William Shakespeare. I can't believe I've said it. This is the first time I've told anyone. The relief! I mean, even if my mother hadn't emotionally blackmailed me, I just assumed that anybody I told would think I was insane. I'm a clone of William Shakespeare! And it's ruined my life. Bill – your Bill – is lucky. He doesn't know, I think. There's no way that he knows. Because imagine trying to live up to that! Imagine, every day, everything you do, or think, or say, let alone write – imagine comparing yourself to Shakespeare! He wouldn't be able to write, he wouldn't be able to do anything. Just like I haven't been able to do anything. I've wasted my whole life! Until I met you, Thandie. I can see why Bill fell in love with you. But you can understand why I had to leave, can't you? Don't you? I couldn't let you saddle your life to me. But you came back to me – Thandie . . .'

Thandie pulled the car up outside a building that Billy didn't recognise.

'Does that mean that you forgive me?' he asked her.

Thandie opened the door. 'Come on, Bill.'

'Billy,' Billy corrected her. He was beginning to suspect that things weren't going quite as well as he had thought.

Nevertheless, he got out of the car and let her lead him into the building, Sal walking behind them. He realised almost immediately that he was in a doctor's surgery. He loathed doctors' surgeries, he was sure he always left them sicker than when he went in.

'We need to see the doctor,' Thandie told the receptionist. 'It's an emergency.'

'We don't,' said Billy. 'It's not.'

The receptionist glanced at Billy. 'Is he still mad?' he asked, scratching his neck tattoo.

'Still mad?' said Thandie.

'He was in earlier.'

'No, I wasn't,' said Billy. 'I've never been here before in my life.'

'Bill,' said Thandie, 'this is our local surgery.'

'I'm not Bill,' said Billy. 'I thought you believed me.'

'Blimey, he really is mad,' said the receptionist. 'I'll let Dr Patel know.' He typed something into his computer. Then he winked at Sal, and grinned. It was the first time any of them had seen him smile. One of his teeth was gold. 'How about you, love?' he said. 'Anything I can help you with today?'

'I'm just here with my brother,' said Sal. 'I'm very worried about him.'

The door to the examination room opened and a man came out with his young daughter. Moments later, the doctor emerged and looked around the waiting room, before hurrying over to where they were standing.

113

'Hello, Thandie, Sal, Bill,' he said. 'Bill, you're back already?'

'I've never been here before and I don't know who you are,' Billy said.

The man turned to Thandie. 'I'm so sorry,' he said. 'He came in earlier and told me that he thought he was going mad – his word, you understand, it's not a medical term – and I sent him home. I thought he was dehydrated.'

'It's all right, Dr Patel, he can be very plausible when he wants to be,' said Thandie.

'I'm not "plausible",' said Billy. 'I'm telling the truth!'

'Perhaps we should step into my office,' said Dr Patel. 'Sal, please could you wait outside.'

'But—' started Sal.

'It's really best we have this conversation with Bill's next of kin only.'

'Thandie's not my next of kin,' said Billy. 'I only met her today.'

But Thandie took Billy's arm and began to guide him towards Dr Patel's office, and short of wrestling her off him, Billy didn't know what to do.

'Excuse me, is that man jumping the queue?' said an old lady at the back of the waiting room.

'I'll make you a nice cup of tea, love,' said the receptionist to Sal. 'Don't worry, your brother will be just fine. Dr Patel will look after him.'

'I'm in here every week and you never offer to make me a cup of tea,' said the old lady.

'I might even have a biscuit for you somewhere,' he said. 'You relax, everything is going to be OK.'

'He's giving her biscuits, now,' announced the old lady. Everyone else in the waiting room pretended to be deeply absorbed in whatever they were doing.

'There's nothing you can do now but wait. Best to think about something else,' the receptionist told Sal.

'I like your tattoo,' Sal said shyly. 'Was it featured in *Skin Deep* magazine?'

'It was!' said the receptionist with another smile.

The old lady rolled her eyes.

Meanwhile, in Dr Patel's office, Billy was trying to explain. 'I'm not mad,' he was saying, 'it's just that the situation is so unusual that anybody hearing about it would conclude that me being mad is likelier than the situation being real.'

'In that case,' said Dr Patel, 'why were you in my office earlier telling me that you are mad?'

'To repeat,' Billy said, 'that wasn't me. That was Bill. William Evans. Thandie's husband. He isn't mad either, he's just not fully apprised of all the facts.'

'The facts?' said Dr Patel.

'He doesn't know that he's a clone.' Billy knew that he had picked the wrong moment to start telling the truth, but now that he'd started he didn't know how to stop.

Dr Patel turned to Thandie and sighed. 'I think we'd better take him in for assessment.'

'In?' said Billy.

'Once he's in, we'll get a better sense of what we're dealing with. He's obviously moving in and out of lucidity in quite a volatile way.'

'I am here,' said Billy. 'You can speak to me directly. What do you mean, "in"?'

'I'll have to call the crisis team,' said Dr Patel, still addressing himself to Thandie, 'but you can wait here until the intake is processed.'

'I'm not going to be "taken" "in" anywhere. There isn't going to be an "intake".'

'Thank you, Dr Patel,' said Thandie. 'I just want what's best for Bill.'

'If you wanted what's best for me, you would talk to me. More to the point, you would listen to me.' Billy looked from Dr Patel to Thandie and back again. 'Are you putting me under section?'

'That's rather a dated term,' said Dr Patel, finally speaking to Billy. 'We prefer to say detained under the Mental Health Act—'

But Billy didn't wait to hear what they preferred to say. He was out of his seat and running away from the doctor's surgery faster than he'd ever imagined that he could.

Even now that evening had fallen, it was still so warm and humid outside that it was like running through soup.

'Sally!' Billy yelled into his phone as he ran. 'Check your bloody voicemail!' As he was yelling this into Sally's voicemail, he knew that the advice was nonsensical. 'They're going to lock me up! Find Bill and tell him everything! They won't believe us until they see me and Bill together!' He hung up, and then, in case she wasn't going to listen to her message, he sent her a text. It was hard to text while running, so he just typed, 'Help they're coming' – apostrophe included, a man needed standards – and then accelerated as much as he could.

Where to hide, where to hide? He barely knew this town. He couldn't head for the station, that was far too obvious. He had no friends he could shelter with, the beach was too open, they'd find him soon enough in any bar. And he couldn't get a cab out of town, he didn't have any money. Steal a car? How the hell do you steal a car? He'd seen people hot-wire cars on TV but that was hardly a how-to guide. Besides, he didn't think adding car theft to his rap sheet was going to help his case much.

He ran hither and thither – hither, Billy vaguely thought, being towards the left, and thither towards the right – up one street and down another. If he got to the edge of town, it occurred to him, maybe he could hitchhike, which he had never done before because it was not safe, and now he would die, and it would be William Evans's fault, for living here. Where was the edge of town? Anywhere other than the sea, he supposed. He picked a direction, more or less at random.

He wasn't sure how long he'd been running when he heard a familiar sound, the chimes of an ice cream van playing 'Oh, I Do Like To Be Beside The Seaside'. When he'd been a kid he'd loved that sound more than anything. Now he thought, no, I don't bloody like to be beside the seaside. I do not like to be beside the sea.

The chimes got louder and louder until the van itself was driving alongside him. The driver leaned over and rolled down his window.

Do I look, thought Billy, lolloping a flailing gallop along the street, sweat glazing his face like lard on a pie, like a man with time to stop for a Mr Frostee?

'Fancy a lift?' said the driver of the ice cream van.

He'll probably murder me and put me in the freezer with the lollies, thought Billy. Probably turn me into a lolly, I'm more sweat than man. 'Yes, please,' he wheezed.

The driver pulled over and Billy crawled into the front beside him.

'Thanks,' he gasped. 'You're a lifesaver.'

He fell back into his seat, taking in huge lungfuls of air.

'Running late, are you?' said the driver as he pulled away. Just in case, Billy tried to figure out how he would describe him to the police. Above average height. Muscular build. Strong, murderer hands. He should have memorised the number plate.

'Can you take me out of town? To anywhere.' He plucked at his seatbelt but he was too exhausted to pull it across himself.

'What's the matter? Why were you running like that?'

'I'd rather not discuss it.'

'Bill, are you all right?'

Of course. Of bloody course. Small towns! Billy thumped the window with his fist. 'Does everybody here know everyone?' he howled. 'Doesn't it drive you all mad? I'm not bloody Bill! I just look like him!'

There was a silence, broken only by the tinny siren song of the van.

'You're the other one,' said the driver eventually.

Billy slowly turned and stared at him. 'The other what?'

'Billy,' said the driver, 'I'm your father.'

17.

When Sal saw Billy running past her, she abandoned her tea and her biscuit and the receptionist with the sexy tattoo, and rushed into Dr Patel's examining room.

'What happened?' she said. 'What did you say to him?'

'I suggested that we take him into a secure environment to figure out what is wrong with him, and he registered his opposition to the idea,' said Dr Patel.

'He ran away,' said Thandie.

'You should have let me stay with him!' said Sal.

'I don't think it would have made any difference,' said Thandie. 'Nobody likes being sectioned, especially if you think that there's nothing wrong with you. So. What should we do now?'

'I think we'd better call the police,' said Dr Patel.

'No!' said Sal.

'I think he's in danger of harming himself or someone else,' said Dr Patel.

'Bill would never harm someone else,' said Sal.

'I agree he'd never hurt anyone,' said Thandie, 'but are you sure that he wouldn't harm himself?'

Sal was filled with terror. 'I'm going to look for him,' she said.

'I don't think that's a good idea,' said Thandie.

'I'll find him before the police will. He's my brother. I know him.'

Dr Patel had picked up the phone, and now waited, the receiver in his hand.

'I don't see what harm there is in Sal going to look for him, but I think we should call the police as well,' Thandie said. 'He's completely lost his grip on reality. Anything could happen to him.'

'Thandie . . . do you think that maybe he's telling the truth?' said Sal. 'That he really is a clone of Shakespeare? I never thought about it before, but he does look like him, and he is very good at writing plays.'

'I know it's less scary to believe him than it is to accept that he's unwell,' said Thandie, 'but you have to think about what's likely. OK, he's a playwright, and he looks like some old paintings that nobody is even certain actually are of Shakespeare – though he does look quite a lot like those paintings . . .' Thandie tailed off.

'That's what makes it such a convincing delusion for him,' said Dr Patel.

'See?' said Thandie. 'We need to trust the doctor.'

'There's obviously a close sense of identification,' continued Dr Patel. 'When I asked him about grandiosity, when he came in earlier, he said that sometimes he thought he might be "Shakespeare-great". Those were his exact words.'

'Isn't what he said to you supposed to be confidential?' Thandie asked.

'I don't know,' said Dr Patel. 'I'm not sure exactly what's covered by the principle of confidentiality, in the case of detention under the Mental Health Act. I mean, he said some far worse things to me that I would definitely not repeat. Especially not to you.'

'Good to know,' said Thandie. 'Why don't you go ahead and call the police?'

While Dr Patel phoned the police and explained the situation, Sal slipped away. Detention under the Mental Health Act. That did not sound good. She'd been in detention plenty at school, and hadn't liked it one bit. Sal didn't know whether Bill was mad or whether he was Shakespeare – and knowing her brother as well as she did, she was increasingly thinking that it was more likely that he was Shakespeare – but she did know that there was no way she was going to let him get detained.

18.

Sally had had a mostly great afternoon. She'd taken what was left of Thandie's twenty quid and gone to the arcade and played lots of games, including that one where you drop 2p coins onto a little shelf and try to make them all fall off the edge, like round copper lemmings, and the one where you try to pick up a cuddly toy with a mechanical claw. Sally enjoyed operating the claw – she briefly wondered whether she should get a job on a building site – and she played the game over and over until she finally managed to lift a toy and drop it down the chute. It was a little plush unicorn, worth far less than the amount of money she'd spent to get it. But she felt a pleasing sense of achievement, and an even more pleasing sense of having made someone very happy when she gave it away to a little boy, who she noticed was staring at it with yearning eyes. After she got bored with the arcade, she'd eaten a hot dog and drunk some fizzy pop, and then she'd stripped down to her underwear and lain on the beach for a while. Some people had stared at her but she didn't care. What was the difference between bra and knickers and a bikini anyway? True, underwear could go saggy or see-through in the water, but she wasn't planning to swim. She'd have had to leave her phone behind, and then she might miss it when Nelson Thomas called.

But Nelson Thomas didn't call. The only person who kept calling and texting was Billy. 'Where are you? We need to go.' 'I'm waiting for you at the station. HURRY.' Sally was sick of being pushed around. So what if Billy wanted to go? What if she didn't want to go? What if she liked this town? What if she wanted to stay? What if they got on the train and then Nelson Thomas called her but the reception was bad and she couldn't hear what he was saying and he was trying to ask her out and even when finally he gave up on talking and sent her a text instead she had to write back saying that she couldn't meet him for fish and chips because she was living in Inverness now? Did Billy think of that?

As the afternoon passed, two things began to dawn on Sally. One was that there was no reason that she had to do what Billy told her to do. She was so accustomed to Billy being the centre of her universe that it had never occurred to her that her universe might have another centre instead. Nelson Thomas, for example. Or even, the centre of her universe could be herself! Was that possible? Could Sally's universe revolve around Sally? She'd never been good at physics, but she liked the sound of it: a Sally Universe, where she could live by the sea and keep all her own money and go to the arcade as often as she wanted.

The second thing that dawned on Sally, though, was that

maybe Nelson Thomas wasn't going to call her after all. This was a slower dawn than the first dawn, a sluggish winter dawn when you're not sure whether the sun is going to make it past the clouds at all, but as Sally replayed every detail of their two conversations in her mind, she kept snagging on the moment that she'd told him that she and the other Sally had been made from the same hair. It was one thing to tell a handsome newsagent owner that you were cloned from William Shakespeare. It was quite another to reveal that you were made from a hair that your mother found on a bus. She was so used to knowing where she came from that she hadn't thought about how it might freak out someone else, someone normal, like Nelson Thomas. Sally, who had been lying outstretched on the sand, soaking up as many sunrays as she could catch, now sat up and hugged her knees to her. Was it possible that this hair revelation had put Nelson Thomas off calling her?

Sally considered going back to the newsagent to explain, but what would she explain, exactly? It's not as if she could tell him that it wasn't true. She wished her mother was there to talk him through it. Her mother had a knack for making things sound clever and important and sensible. Her mother could sell a hair-clone, no problem. But her mother, thought Sally, was a long way away. (Sally was wrong. Her mother was currently as close to Sally as she had been in years, being told by a police officer that her case would be processed any minute now, so please shut up.) Maybe she should call her. Billy said never to call her. But Billy – Billy who had insisted that they should not be separated – wasn't here now.

Sally picked up her phone and examined it, just in case she had put it on silent by mistake and Nelson Thomas had called without her noticing. She hadn't, and he hadn't. She looked up her mother's number. Her finger hovered above it. Billy, she knew, would be outraged. He had vowed that they would only see their mother again once he had a play in the West End, to prove her wrong – although as Sally saw it, this would in fact prove their mother right. But Sally, while loyal, was beginning to question whether Billy was ever going to have a play in the West End, though this was certainly the West End's loss. And what did any of that have to do with her anyway?

As she held her phone, her dial finger quivering with indecision, it suddenly rang and, in shock, Sally dropped it face down in the sand. Nelson Thomas, she thought. She picked it up with shaking hands and tried to brush the sand off it. But it was Billy, of course. She felt even angrier with Billy for not being Nelson. She let the phone ring itself to voicemail. Then she let the voicemail beep without checking it. Grudgingly, though, she did read the text message that followed.

'Help they're coming'

Despite the warm evening, Sally felt a cold chill. 'Help they're coming' could not be anything good. Her battery was low, and she'd been saving it for Nelson Thomas, but Billy was in trouble. She forgot Nelson in a blink. She dialled up her voicemail and listened to the messages he'd left her. The first few weren't so different from the grumpy texts he'd sent about waiting at the station, but in the last one, he was obviously running, and terrified. 'They're going to lock me up,' he'd said, but he didn't say who, or why. All she knew from the message was that Bill was the only one who could help him, and she was the only one who could find Bill.

She put on her clothes as fast as she could. Her T-shirt was inside out and her jeans were full of sand but she didn't care. She tried to run while putting her shoes on and ended up flat on her face on the beach. She pulled herself up, somehow got her shoes on and kept going.

She tore to the B&B, the only place that she knew Bill might have gone to, took the stairs two at a time, but when she got to the top, Bill's – or Billy's – room was empty, save the suitcase and the clothes and books piled up on the floor. She ran back down the stairs again, but her thoughts were racing even faster than she was. Where could she find Bill? How? What would happen to Billy if she didn't find him?

Reaching the street, she paused, looking to the left and the right, trying to figure out where Bill might have gone. Suddenly she noticed a familiar figure standing on a doorstep a few houses down, talking to a man who shook his head and closed the door. A very familiar figure. It was her. Herself. That is to say, Other Sally.

'Other Sally!' she yelled. 'Other Sally! It's me! Sally! Real Sally!'

Other Sally turned to her and gasped. Sally wasn't close enough to hear her gasp, but she knew that she must have, because Sally would have gasped if she'd been in Other Sally's position. If it wasn't a gasp it was a small cough. Her mouth was open anyway.

Quite out of breath by now, Sally ran over to her double, who was also running down the stairs and towards her. They stopped and stared at one another. The short, thickset legs that they both liked even though they weren't long, skinny model legs because they made them feel strong and cute like a pony; the torso with one shoulder sloped slightly lower than the other which they didn't like because it meant they got back pain if they slept in a funny position; the blonde hair, the same colour as that one from the bus seat, tucked back behind ears shaped like little pink shells which they both considered to be their best feature; the matching expressions of shock tinged with delight. Right now the only real difference in their appearances was that Sally had her T-shirt on inside out.

'You're me,' said Sally.

'I'm you,' said Sal.

Then they both burst into huge smiles and hugged. 'This is so cool!' they said together.

'OK,' said Sally. 'This is totally amazing and the best thing that's ever happened in my life and I can't wait to talk to you for hours and hours and hours and find out if you also get that weird pain in your left shoulder when you've eaten too much, because I've never met anybody else who does, but it's going to have to wait because I got a message from my brother Billy saying he's in trouble and he urgently needs our help.'

'I knew Bill was telling the truth!' said Sal. Then she stopped and her lips moved briefly while she figured something out. 'Oh, wait, it was Other Bill who was telling the truth, but that's the same as Bill telling the truth because Bill would have told the truth if it had been Bill.'

'Exactly!' said Sally.

'But that means it's Other Bill who's in trouble, which means that I'm not going to find him because Real Bill's the one who told me that he's staying in a B&B, but Other Bill's the one who ran away and he could be anywhere else right now. I've just knocked on the doors of seven B&Bs when I should have been anywhere else!'

'That's OK because Real Billy phoned me and told me that I need to find Other Billy, but he didn't say why.'

'It's because Other Bill told the doctor that he's a clone and the doctor thinks he's mad and wants to lock him up and the only way that he can prove that he's telling the truth is to find Real Bill, only I don't know where Real Bill is, and Other Bill has run away.'

'So we need to find them both,' said Sally. 'OK, Real Billy's not at the B&B and is hiding somewhere, and Other Billy isn't at the B&B either. Do you know where else Other Billy might be?'

'I can think of somewhere,' said Sal. She began to lead the way. 'I do get the shoulder thing, by the way,' she added.

'I don't know why Real Billy said it would be confusing if the clones got together,' said Sally, following her. 'It all seems totally straightforward to me.'

19.

Bill had taken Dr Patel's advice with a pinch of salt. Also some ketchup. He'd gone to the Boar's Head and ordered a burger with fries and a pint of beer. Beer had alcohol in it, true, but it was also very refreshing and probably excellent for rehydration, and nobody ever took doctors' advice completely anyway. They knew that when they gave you the advice, which was why it was always extra demanding – they expected you to only do half of it at most. Besides, if there was ever a day to ignore your doctor's advice on alcohol consumption, today was it.

Sal was trying to phone him but he wanted to figure out his next move before he spoke to her. Did anyone ever pick up their phone any more? Next time he wrote a play, he was going to make it all about people ignoring their phones. Maybe there could be a story in which someone had to pass on a message about something really important, a matter of life or death, and the message is missed because that person doesn't pick up their phone ... There was definitely something in that.

On a dramatic level, Bill was disappointed to discover that he wasn't mad – it was hard to make good art from dehydration and mild anxiety – but on a human level he was relieved. Of all the things he loved in the world, the inside of his own head was his favourite. Of course, he was saddened by the end of his marriage. Of course, he was grieving the loss of his relationship with Anthony. But he knew he would recover from both of these blows. The loss of his ability to think, his ability to write, that would be unendurable. Thandie had always accused him of loving his work more than he loved her. He should apologise to her for ever having denied it.

Now, though, he had more pressing issues to resolve. He couldn't go home; he refused to go back to that mouldy-carpeted hellhole of a B&B. He had a brief, vivid fantasy of going and living in the forest by himself, but there weren't any proper forests in the UK any more, just pretty little woods with nature trails and viewing platforms, or lifeless, regimented tree factories you weren't allowed to trespass in anyway. And romantic as the notion of himself as an arboreal hermit was, it would make more sense to go and stay with his dad until he and Thandie figured out the terms of the divorce. He called his dad, but he wasn't picking up his landline, and his mobile inevitably went straight through to voicemail. Bill's father had never really adapted to mobile phones. He treated his as some kind of portable phone box, switched off unless he himself wanted to make a call. It never seemed to occur to him that somebody else might want to phone him. Bill decided to wait until later, when his dad was likelier to be home.

Wait until later. There was a seductive pull in that. Sometimes it made sense to put off all of life's questions and retreat to the fat salt of a chip, the sharpness of beer.

And then Sal walked in. And then Sal walked in.

Two Sals.

Two Sals, or this was one of the delusions Dr Patel had asked him about.

No, the barmaid had seen them and dropped a glass. There were definitely two Sals. One of whom had her T-shirt on inside out. This explained everything. No. This explained almost everything, except—

'There's two of me too, isn't there?' he said, as he jumped up to meet them. 'Two of you, two of me. Where's the other me? Which one of you is Sal? No, of course, it's you.' He hugged Sal, the correct one, with her T-shirt on the right way round.

'How can you tell?' said Sal.

'I just . . . you're my sister. Although, I suppose, so are you?' he said to Sally.

'I'm Sally,' said Sally.

'It's a bit more complicated than brothers and sisters,' said Sal. 'We'll explain it to you, but we don't have a lot of time.'

'But I think you should probably sit down and drink your beer while we tell you,' said Sally.

Bill sat down again and, for what it was worth, had a sip of beer. Sal and Sally exchanged a look, in which some wordless information also seemed to get transmitted.

'OK,' said Sal, 'I'll be the one who tells you. But we're in a bit of a hurry, so I can't do all the bits that prepare you for it

135

like you do when you've got big news for me. You're a clone of William Shakespeare, and—'

'William Shakespeare?' said Bill.

'Yes. You know, the playwright.'

'William Shakespeare,' Bill said again. He found that he was standing up. He somehow felt that he needed to fill up more space. 'I'm Shakespeare.'

'Well, sort of,' said Sal. 'But—'

'That's right,' said Bill. He felt dazed, and yet he was fast becoming suffused with a sense of certainty. 'Of course, that's right. It's insane but it's right. And it's not like I knew, obviously not, but, now that you say it – yes. You know, reading his plays, I always felt this affinity – like he'd written them for me – like I could have written them myself. I always thought that there was a special connection between us. But I never said so because I would have sounded – I don't know – pretentious – a lunatic . . .' Bill felt as if he'd opened a hidden door in his mind, into a place where everything essential for his understanding of himself had been concealed. And not just his own understanding of himself, but everyone else's understanding of him too. He barked a laugh. 'So I'm not "derivative"! I'm the original! Ha! The *Daily Telegraph* can suck my balls.'

'I'm sure they'd be happy to, later,' said Sally, 'but my brother Billy, who is also a clone of Shakespeare—'

This was less pleasing to hear. 'How many of us are there?' said Bill.

Sal and Sally shrugged with an identical gesture. 'I don't

know. My mum never even said there was more than one of us,' said Sally.

'And what about you two? Who are you clones of? Jane Austen? Marie Curie?'

Sally shifted uncomfortably. 'We're the control group,' she said. 'But the thing is, we have to hurry, because Billy—'

'Who else knows?' said Bill.

'Um . . . My mum and Billy, obviously. And today Billy told – er . . .?'

'Thandie and Dr Patel,' said Sal. 'And then Dr Patel told the police.'

'The police? Why did he tell the police?'

'That's what we've been trying to tell you,' said Sal.

But before Sal could finish, two police officers came into the pub, and began to make their way over to Bill's table.

'I guess they can tell me themselves,' said Bill.

20.

The man who called himself Billy's father pulled over in a side street.

'Hopefully, there won't be too many customers,' he said, 'but if they come, I'll have to serve them. Turning children away from an ice cream van when you're inside it is too cruel.'

'Yes, you're obviously the kind of man who hates letting children down, Father who abandoned me as a baby and whom I have never heard from or about in the whole of my life before now.'

'You have a point there.' Billy's so-called father nodded. 'I'm sure you're very angry with me, and with good reason. But I'll tell you anything that you want to know.'

'All right then,' said Billy, 'Let's see ... How about this: what's your name?'

'That's a good question. I go by Madoc Evans. But my real name is Maximilian van der Vegte. A bit of a mouthful, and very easy to trace, though it's a good online-banking password. Madoc Evans is a better name to hide with. It sounds Welsh, you see. If you tell people you're Welsh, they just go on about

139

sheep and Tom Jones and call you Boyo and never ask you any questions. Also I am a mad doc. So there's a little joke in there.'

'It's not funny.'

'No, I suppose not.'

'You admit you were hiding, then.'

'Yes, but not from you.'

'And yet I might never have found you.'

'That's true.'

'99 Flake please.'

It was a small voice from an even smaller child outside the window of the van. Madoc got up and served the child his ice cream. The child trotted away with a big grin.

'Do you fancy one?' he said to Billy afterwards.

'Sure,' he said. 'With two flakes. And chocolate sauce.'

'I hear that's how Shakespeare liked his,' said Madoc.

'Also not funny.'

'Sorry.'

'What were you thinking?'

'I was just trying to lighten the mood.'

'No. What were you thinking when you decided to make me?'

'Ah.'

Madoc finished swirling the chocolate sauce onto the ice cream and stuck in the two flakes. He handed it to Billy and climbed back into the front seat.

'I was ambitious in those days. And selfish. I imagined myself as the most famous scientist in the world. Human cloning is an extremely complex procedure, but with Eleanor I thought I might be able to make it happen—'

'Because she could carry the babies?'

'No, no, that's not important. Half the population has a womb. It's that she's a much better scientist than I am. It was a lab match, not a love match, you understand. But she wanted more, she was greedy; it wasn't enough for her to learn the secrets of the body, she wanted the mind as well. And when she outlined her plan, it was tempting, too tempting, how could I resist the opportunity to meet William Shakespeare himself—'

'Hello? A rocket and a Calippo please.'

Billy watched Madoc get up again and serve his customers, a sunburned woman with a little girl, maybe five or six. Her face lit up as her mother handed her the Calippo.

'Maybe it would make more sense if you joined me back here,' said Madoc.

Billy went into the body of the van with his father. There wasn't a lot of room back there between the ice cream machine, the drinks fridge and the freezer chest, but they managed to squeeze in. Billy felt a thrill of being allowed somewhere secret and forbidden. It reminded him of how he felt the first time he went behind the scenes in a theatre.

'So,' he said, 'Shakespeare.'

'Yes. It was a terrible thing to do. I think I realised the moment the two of you were born, how terrible it was. You weren't William Shakespeare, you were just two little babies. Loud babies. You liked expressing yourselves, is what Eleanor said. But I buried my misgivings, it was just so exciting that we had succeeded. Human clones! The first in the world! The idea from the start was to bring you up separately. One knowing, one not knowing. One nature, one nurture. At first I lived with Bill nearby, while Eleanor worked on the control group.'

'Sally. Her name is – their names are – Sally.'

'We argued over the names. I wanted different ones for all of you. But Eleanor thought that for the "nurture" half of the experiment to succeed, you needed to be called William. And she said that the comparison wouldn't work unless my child was called William too, that the results might be skewed. Who knows what influence a name has on a person? In the end I agreed. For science. Then for the control, I wanted Rose. Another stupid joke. Because that which we call a rose by any other name . . .'

'So why Sally?'

'It's Eleanor's mother's name. She had to cut off all contact with her relatives – too many complications – and she missed them. She had to be very tough, Eleanor. She is not completely bad as a person. Or if she is, there are reasons. I could still communicate with my family; my babies were "normal". I made up a story about a wife who left me. I based her heavily on Eleanor. A fellow scientist who hurt me so badly I gave up my career, changed my name. Well. Not important. At first I went along with the plan. I went away with Bill and Sal, left you and Sally to be raised by Eleanor, moved far enough away that you would never meet by chance. We thought. But I started feeling it was wrong to leave you two behind the moment I closed the car door. Maybe even before. You weren't my flesh and blood, we weren't in any way related; I told myself I had nothing to feel guilty about. And yet. I knew. Eleanor and I wrote to each other, sent each other our observations about the subjects, that is, the children, how they – you – were developing. My Bill and Sal were normal kids – well, Bill was never exactly "normal", he had a precocious intellect from the start, but they had normal childhoods, normal development, they thrived. And Sally, your Sally, was a happy child. But you. Eleanor told me that you were moody, difficult, withdrawn. She thought maybe that was natural, the sign of creativity, but I knew that it had to be from the pressure you were under. Because Bill was so doing so well, you see. I felt sick about what we had done. I stopped sending Eleanor updates, stopped all my scientific observations of the children, changed our names, moved again. Our arrangement had originally been that I would tell Bill and Sal everything once Sal was eighteen and Bill twenty-one, so that they could choose how to make their way in the world as adults, but I never did. I didn't want to rob them of their innocence, their chance to just be people, nothing special, just people like anybody else.'

'What about my chance?'

'It was too late for you.'

As Billy's soul tore into myriad tiny pieces, a large group of kids arrived at the van and started to place their orders. There were so many of them waiting that eventually Billy began to help Madoc serve them. He found that it made him feel better. There was something so simple and satisfying about it, handing

143

over the ice creams and seeing the children smile. Madoc appeared to notice the effect the work was having on him.

'Nice, isn't it?' he said. 'Making people happy. I could have carried on as a scientist, I was one of the best, but I'd had enough of playing god. After causing all that pain, I wanted to do something that increased the amount of joy in the world. This seemed like a good way to do it.'

Billy closed the freezer and went back into the front seat. Presently, Madoc joined him.

'I thought of coming for you, many times,' he said. 'And I so nearly did. But I was always afraid.'

'Afraid of what?'

'That Eleanor would come for my Bill and my Sal, and ruin their lives the way I'd already ruined yours. So I hid. I thought that at least I had saved two of you. And I hoped that I was wrong, that you might be content, fulfilled. Once we had the internet, once I thought the kids were resilient enough to withstand Eleanor if she tracked us down in return, I did look you up, over and over, but I never found you. I wondered if you also changed your name.'

'No. But I never did anything google-able.'

'I'm so sorry for everything I've done to you,' said Madoc. 'If you can, I was hoping you might one day forgive me. I'm still working on forgiving myself.'

Billy was about to say that he never would, but his phone rang in his pocket. He felt relieved. He wasn't sure whether he'd have been telling the truth.

'I hate those things,' said Madoc.

'So do I,' said Billy. 'I never answer it.' But he pulled out the phone anyway. 'Oh, I definitely need to take this. Sally?'

'Billy,' said Sally at the other end, 'Other Billy's been arrested! They think you're both the same person, and they're going to put him in detention. I explained everything to him before the police got there, but that means he told them about there being two of you and that both of you are Shakespeare, and that made it all worse. Other Sally's gone with him to the police station. Oh, I met Other Sally. She's cool. What do you want me to do?'

I could leave now, thought Billy. Nobody's looking for me any more. I'm sure Madoc can get Bill out of the loony bin. And I don't owe him anything, we've never even met. Sally would be fine here, she could work in that newsagent she's got her heart set on. Northern Ireland. The Giant's Causeway. Always wanted to see the Giant's Causeway.

'How fast does this thing go?' he asked Madoc.

21.

Finally Eleanor was being discharged, with a caution, which really pissed her off. A caution against what? Kicking further traffic wardens? Wasn't being kicked an occupational hazard of being a traffic warden? If they didn't want to be kicked, they should go into the kind of job that didn't involve annoying members of the general public. The police called it 'assault', but it was just nature. She could have given them a lecture on nature if she'd wanted to. She probably had slides on her phone. But it had been a long day, the hottest day of the year, and she'd spent it all in some disgusting cell that smelled of urine and had no natural light or air but still managed to be as hot as Hades. They'd have kept her in all night if she hadn't 'confessed'. In her head she put the confession into inverted commas, because she didn't really mean it, even though, OK, she *had* actually kicked that traffic warden.

There was loads of paperwork. She had to give a statement, which was copied down by some barely literate officer, and then she had to read it and sign it over and over and over to say that she agreed with it. Then there was some further procedure around the administration of the caution itself, and then finally a seemingly endless kerfuffle to get her possessions back. Waiting at the front desk, in her stockinged feet, she thought that the police force itself should be arrested, for wasting police time.

She drummed her fingers on the desk as she waited. She wasn't alone in the station. There were a few orange plastic chairs in the lobby area, and fidgeting on one was an attractive, if somewhat overweight, black woman, beside a slightly older Asian man who looked far calmer, possibly even slightly bored. The woman kept checking her phone, which irritated Eleanor because she still didn't have her own phone back.

Then the doors to the station opened and two police officers came in, with a young man and a younger woman whom Eleanor recognised instantly. She frantically began to prepare a story, but beyond a glance when they first entered, they didn't react to her at all. Eleanor realised that these must be the other pair of clones – she knew they lived in this town, that was why she had come here after all – and yet she couldn't fight her instinct that they must, somehow, know who she was.

The resemblance really was uncanny. Of course their bodies looked the same. But the way they held themselves, their facial expressions, the way they walked – how many times had she told Sally to stand up straight? They even had the same hair-cuts (as far as Eleanor could recall), the same style of clothing. For a moment she wanted to rush over and embrace them, but all along her intention had been to observe them in secret, and there was no reason why that should change now, even if –

especially if – they had just been arrested. Besides, it would hardly make a good impression on them, meeting her like this. She could wait. Eleanor pushed her feelings as far down as they would go. She was not their mother. She was a scientist.

The fat woman jumped up from her seat and ran to Billy – to Bill, Eleanor corrected herself. She was surprisingly nimble.

'I'm sorry, Bill,' she said, 'but there's no other way for you to get the help you need.'

'Don't apologise to me,' said Bill (his voice exactly like Billy's). 'It's Billy you should be apologising to.'

Now Eleanor was truly astonished. Somehow Bill and Billy had made contact! Exactly how much did he know? Had Maximilian told him everything? Perhaps Bill had emailed Billy around the same time that he had emailed her, wanting to make contact with, as he put it, his 'birth mother'. Which was quite insulting, given that he had no way of knowing that his 'genetic mother' had died in 1608.

'I think we should probably take this into one of the interview rooms,' said the Asian man. 'I've called for someone from the mental health team, and they should be here soon.'

Mental health? Now this was satisfying. Maximilian had always been so insistent that his children were models of perfect development.

'There's nothing wrong with my mental health,' said Bill – well, he would say that, wouldn't he?

'Bill . . .' started the fat woman, presumably a girlfriend – no, she was wearing a wedding ring. A wife! Eleanor surreptitiously examined her. Fat women always had good skin, so it was hard to guess her age, but she didn't look much older than Bill, perhaps younger, even. Not an Anne Hathaway, then. Later, once she had made Bill's acquaintance and set up a formal interview, she could ask him whether as a youth he'd ever had a physical relationship with an older woman. Modern contraception would presumably have prevented any accidental pregnancies. Hopefully, Bill would be more mature than Billy when it came to the interview. Billy had always been so reticent in answering questions about his sexual encounters.

'Here are your things,' the officer behind the counter said to her. 'You can go now.'

'Finally,' said Eleanor. But she had no intention of leaving. She took her shoes and put them on as slowly as she could.

'He's telling the truth,' Sal said. 'There's two of him. They're clones.'

At that word, everyone in the station was gripped. Now Eleanor didn't have to feign an excuse to stick around. It would seem like natural curiosity.

'Sal, I admire your loyalty to Bill, but you're not helping him by buying into his delusions,' said Bill's wife. 'He needs professional care.'

They were sectioning him for claiming to be a clone! Should she step in and confirm his story? She could end the confusion in a matter of moments. But she would find out more by staying silent.

'But it's true!' Sal was saying.

'How do you know?' said Bill's wife. 'Have you seen this other Bill?'

'No,' said Sal, 'but I've seen the other me.'

Eleanor gasped, but fortunately, so did the Asian doctor or whatever he was, so nobody noticed. Sal had met Sally! Was it possible that Billy and Sally were here, now, in this town?

'The other . . . you?'

'Yes, Thandie,' said Sal. 'And I'm definitely not mad so Bill isn't either. I don't know why everyone thinks it's so weird. Barbra Streisand had her dog cloned, and if they can do that, they can do people, and they did Bill and me. Other Sal explained everything to us.'

'Other Sal?'

'The other me. We're made from the same hair. Just a normal hair. But they made Bill and Other Bill out of one of Shakespeare's teeth!'

'Sal, I know that you want to support your brother . . .' The woman called Thandie put a hand on Sal's shoulder.

It began to occur to Eleanor that inside a police station was not the best place for her to be, should these revelations go much further. She gathered up the rest of the possessions that the desk clerk had returned to her and made her way, as casually as she could, to the front door of the police station. Just before she could leave, though, the door opened, and in came Sally.

'Mum!' she cried, and threw her arms around Eleanor.

Eleanor had never liked being hugged. She patted Sally a couple of times on the back. 'Yes, yes, it's me,' she said. 'Why have you got your T-shirt on inside out? Don't you ever look in the mirror?'

'This is my mother,' Sally told the room. 'She's the one who made us!'

Now all eyes were on Eleanor.

'Well, now that that's all cleared up, I'll be on my way,' she said.

Immediately, there was a chorus of dissent. Eleanor tried to edge to the door, but Sally had a firm grip on her arm.

'But, Mum, I haven't seen you for five years, you can't just leave,' she was saying. 'And don't you want to meet Other Billy and Other Sally? You made them too! And they're really nice! Where's Billy? I thought he'd be here!'

Sally tried to drag her over to the others, who were all asking questions at once.

'Well, I suppose I do have time for a quick chat,' said Eleanor, prying Sally's fingers away. 'Why don't we go somewhere together? There must be one cafe in this town that has a decent coffee machine.'

'So you're Eleanor Anderson,' said Bill, stepping into her path. 'My long-lost mother. I emailed you a few weeks ago. You didn't reply. And yet here you are in my home town. What a coincidence. Tell me, is there any particular reason you were happy to watch me get carted off to a loony bin when you could have intervened at any time and explained the whole situation?'

'We don't say loony bin,' said the doctor.

'I think we'd all appreciate some clarification,' said Bill's wife.

'Well, I am Sally's mother, of course,' Eleanor told them. 'And Sal's. They're twins. And I'm, ah, Bill's mother too, yes. A shame we didn't meet under other circumstances. But as for all of this talk of cloning . . .'

Then the door opened again.

22.

'A family reunion,' said Billy. 'Perfect.'

He should have been surprised to see Eleanor, but he was long past anything surprising him today. If another Eleanor had stepped out from behind her, he would merely have shrugged.

'It's not impossible to have two sets of identical twins in the same family,' Eleanor said.

'And hello to you too,' Billy said.

He looked around the police station: at his mother, his (for want of a better word) father, the two Sallies and Thandie, who looked like she was about to keel over from shock. And there he was: William Evans. Scratching his chin the way Billy did when he felt nervous. Billy realised that he was also scratching his chin. They both dropped their hands at once. It was like looking into one of those distorting mirrors at a fairground, except that instead of making him look grotesque, this reflection made him look successful. At least William Evans was just as bald as he was.

'I'm Bill,' said William Evans, holding out his hand.

'Billy.'

They shook hands for a moment. Then Bill pulled Billy in and hugged him. Billy resisted briefly, then gave into it.

'This is incredible,' said Bill. 'I can hardly begin to process it.'

'You had no idea?' said Billy.

'None. Although I do keep writing twins into my plays. Maybe this is why. A long-buried memory of you.'

'I didn't know about you either. Mum always said there was just one of me.'

They both turned and faced Eleanor.

'Statistically, it's only a one in three thousand chance,' said Eleanor. 'Two sets of identical twins . . .'

'I think it's time we told the truth,' said Madoc said to her.

'Look at where we are,' Eleanor hissed.

'Look at who is here,' Madoc replied. He raised his voice. 'Excuse me, everyone. These people are clones. This woman and I made them. We have all kinds of evidence to prove it, should that be required. Nobody is mad, and nobody should be sectioned. Our apologies for all the harm we have done. I for one certainly regret it.' He looked pointedly at Eleanor.

Dr Patel shuffled into a corner. Billy heard him speaking into his phone: 'I won't be needing you after all. False alarm. Yes, it turned out they were clones after all. I know, I'm surprised too.'

One of the police officers who had brought Bill in said to the desk sergeant, 'If we arrest them for human cloning, we're going to have to interview all of these people as witnesses, aren't we?'

'Is human cloning illegal?' said the desk sergeant.

'Yes, I think so,' said the other arresting officer. 'It's not something that comes up a lot.'

'We'll have to interview them all,' repeated the first officer, 'and we'll have to process that woman again.'

They all looked over at Eleanor.

'Maybe we can just let them go,' said the desk sergeant. 'I mean, it's not like we're catching them in the act of cloning right now.'

'Would you mind doing me a favour?' Bill said to Billy, getting out his phone. He put his arm around Billy's shoulders and took a photo of the two of them together. Then he texted it to Anthony. He wrote: 'I love you. Do you still love me?'

'Don't you think this would make a wonderful play?' he said. 'Maybe without the cloning part, nobody would ever believe that. But two sets of long lost twins, mistaken for one another, all set in one day in a seaside town . . .'

Billy nodded, watching him more than he was listening to him. We're not the same person, he thought. We've got the same body, but we haven't lived the same life. We've got the same brain, but we haven't got the same mind. There is no other me. He laughed suddenly and threw his arms around his brother.

'We already hugged!' said Bill, laughing an identical laugh.

'Yes, but this time I mean it,' said Billy.

'So, yeah,' he could hear Sally explaining to Sal, 'I think he did like me, but I messed it up by telling him about how we were both made out of hair, I think he thought I was nuts. But if you come to the newsagent with me, then he'll see that there really are two of me, and then maybe he'll want to call me. Except he won't need to call me, because I'll be standing right there.'

'Does he have any tattoos?' said Sal.

The door to the station opened again. 'Oh, God,' said the desk sergeant, 'what now?'

Everyone looked to see who had come in.

'For crying out loud,' said Eleanor. 'I admitted kicking you, OK? What more do you want?'

Anthony rolled his eyes. 'I'm not here to see you.'

He walked over to Billy and kissed him.

'Wrong clone,' said Billy, disengaging himself.

'How did you know I was here?' said Bill.

'I was here for ages this morning giving a statement, and I recognised the "Don't Drink and Drive" poster behind your heads,' Anthony said. 'And yes, I do love you.' He kissed the correct clone. 'By the way,' he added, 'there's an ice cream van illegally parked outside. I haven't ticketed it. I do have a soul.'

With Bill happily in the clutches of his lover, Madoc talking to the two Sallies with great excitement and Eleanor watching the whole scene somewhat sadly, Billy made his way over to Thandie, who had sunk into a seat and was shaking her head. He sat down beside her.

'I've got so many thoughts and they're all trying to get out at the same time,' said Thandie. 'It's like a traffic jam. I don't think I can say anything to you just yet.'

'Well then, let me go first,' said Billy. He looked for the exact right words to say. Then he thought, screw the exact right words. 'I was a total shit,' he said. 'I told myself it was OK because you didn't know I wasn't him, but it wasn't OK. I'm sorry. The thing is, I'm not a very good person. I don't think I ever have been. Coming back here might be the first time I have ever done the right thing. I have to say I kind of like it.' He paused. 'You know which one I am, right? I'm the other one. Not your husband.'

'Yes, I know,' said Thandie. 'The two of you are actually pretty different.'

'Anyway, like I said, I'm sorry. I know that's not enough. I wish I hadn't slept with you. Even though – no, I still wish I hadn't. We can tell the police if you like. I'll admit everything. We're in the right place for it.'

'No need for that,' said Thandie. 'I'm not saying I forgive you. But these are unusual circumstances.'

They sat in silence for a little while. Then Billy said, 'If things had been different, I might have asked you to dinner.'

'If things had been different, I might have said yes.' Thandie half smiled, then looked away. 'But they're not different. And even if they were, I don't think I can ever date a writer again. Not after being married to Shakespeare.'

'But I'm not a writer,' said Billy.

'Aren't you?' said Thandie.

'No.'

'So what are you?'

Billy smiled. 'I have absolutely no idea.'

A Note on the Author

Marie Phillips is the author of the international bestseller *Gods Behaving Badly* and *The Table of Less Valued Knights*, which was longlisted for the Baileys Prize. With Robert Hudson, she wrote the BBC Radio 4 series *Warhorses of Letters* and *Some Hay in a Manger*. Under the name Vanessa Parody, she co-wrote *Fifty Shelves of Grey*.

Unbound
Liberating ideas

Unbound is the world's first crowdfunding publisher, established in 2011.

We believe that wonderful things can happen when you clear a path for people who share a passion. That's why we've built a platform that brings together readers and authors to crowdfund books they believe in – and give fresh ideas which don't fit the traditional mould the chance they deserve.

This book is in your hands because readers made it possible. Everyone who pledged their support is listed below. Join them by visiting unbound.com and supporting a book today.

Hilary Adamson

Naomi Alderman

Neil Appleton

Paul Arman

Isabelle Arrighi

Simon Arthur

Daan Bakker

Lucy Barlow

Rachael Beale

Anoushka Beazley

Alex Bellos

Liz Bickerdike

Rose Biggin

Paulien Bom

BJ Boulter

Adam Bowie

Thorsten Brandt

Elysia Brenner

Alicia Breton Ferrer

Alice Broadribb

Thomas Brockwell

Claire Broughton

Stephen Brown

Alison Bullock

Leo Burley

Glenn Burton

Stephanie Butland

Victoria C-f

Steven Canny

Andrea Cartier

Ana Cecilia

Paul Chesters

Karen Cinnamon

Rosemary Clarke

Nicola Cloherty

Lucy Coats

Laurence Colchester

Matt Collins

Amy Cooper

Ben Crewe

Amy Crocker

Molly Crockett

Connie Cullen

Heather Culpin

Rishi Dastidar

E R Andrew Davis

Miranda Dickinson

Juliet Drysdale

Tors Duce

Brittany Duncan

Kathryn Eastman

Sharon Eckman

Jean Edelstein

Lynn Enright

Rebekah Fearnside

Aya Ferguson

Kate Ferguson

Erin Fields

Monique Fikse

Nicola Foster

Sarah Franklin

Naomi Frisby

Zoe Fritz

Téa García-Huidobro C.

Mark Garrison

Annabel Gaskell

Adele Geras

Julia Gibby

Teresa Giles

Kerry Glencorse

Melanie Gow

Zoe Greaves

Rose Green
Sarah Grochala
Lia Hadley
Michael Harpur
Shelley Harris
Lucy Head
Daniel Hillel-Tuch
Chantal Hintze
Rachel Holdsworth
Stephen Hoppe
Chloë Houston Mandy
Kerry Hudson
Robert Hudson
Bahman and Roya Irvani
Rivka Isaacson
Ruth James
Isabelle Janvrin
Julia Jarman
Sally Johnston
Claire Jolliffe
Lyndon Jones
Nick Jordan
Sadakat Kadri
Karen Kao
Andrew Kaufman
Valerie Keller
Linda Kennedy
Dan Kieran

Tiffany King
Maria King-Koroleva
Doreen Knight
Linda Knowles
Richard Kramer
Pierre L'Allier
Anne La Berge
Susie Lamb
Agnes Lammers
Christine Lammers
David Lammers
Hadewych Lammers
Deborah Lee
Tom Lee
Kirsten Lester
Hugh Lewis
Chris Limb
Melissa Loddo
Helen Lovett
Anna Lowman
Shona Mackintosh
Caroline Maclean
Madoc
Lisa Maechling
Catherine Makin
Catherine Manning
Izzy Mant
Katie Martin

Martin McKee

Jane McPhee

Rebecca McPhee

Liz Mermin

Tomma Mesch

Colette Milward

John Mitchinson

Elizabeth Mohr

Guy Oscar Morris

Tarek Mouganie

Amy Mustill

Caroline Mustill

Ollie Mustill

Carlo Navato

ETori NotMine

Par Olsson

Richard Osman

Scott Pack

Gordon Peake

Susannah Pearse

Dan Peters

Christylle Phillips

Rebecca Phillips Marques

Caroline Phipps-Urch

Anna Pillay

Justin Pollard

Hannah Powley

Franbert Poyet

Helen Quigley

Amber Rahim

Helen Reid

Clive Richardson

Jo Richardson

Wyn Roberts

Frances Robinson

Patrick Robinson

Emily Roche

Al Roots

Stephanie Rose

Jean-Yves Rouffiac

Julie Rouffiac

Sophie Rouffiac

Helen Rudd

Kortni Rudge

Lisa Rull

Jonathan Ruppin

Alex Ruston

Sarah Salway

Anna Savory

Carol Sayles

Alexandra Scannell

Robyn Scott

Myra Sefton

Safia Shah

Tahir Shah

Miki Shaw

Amy Shindler
Cherry Siddall
Marina Simmons
Jan Smedh
Jennie Smith
Mark Smith
Masa Spaan
Jen Spencer
Sally Stares
Anna Steward
Christopher Stuart
Elizabeth Swann
Flora Swartland
Jane Swartland
Michael Swartland
Perdita Swift
Andy Taylor
Claire Taylor
Heleen Terwijn
Eliana Tomkins
Susannah Tomkins
Richard Tracey

Karen Usher
Ellen Utrecht
Michel van Es
Jonathan Wakeham
Jess Waldura
Christopher Walker
Simone Warner
Ruth Waterton
Miss Wells
Mike Westcott
Frances Wheare
Douglas Whiteside
Jane Whittaker
Deborah Whitworth
Jasper Wight
Kate Williams
Rebecca Wober
Gretchen Woelfle
Philip Womack
Ed Woodcock
Takako Yamamura
Peter Young